Fat Liar

....

Chloe Reeves

Contents

200 Going On 300

The young man walks through the hallway of his North Carolina high school. The bell rings for fourth period as he frantically looks through his locker. He blue eyes avoiding everyone in the hallway. His books cuddle up into his not so flat chest. His not so skinny arms hide under the blue sleeves of the heavy hoodie he's wearing in the middle of May. He's glad school's almost out. He didn't like people, and people didn't like him. Before walking into his classroom he accidentally runs into someone. They mumble "fat ass" under their breath as they walk away. The boy shakes his head and tries to ignore it. He walks into the classroom, just before the late bell rings. "You're cutting it short Mr. Dennis," the teacher groans and clicks his pen. Children in the class whisper, and an overthinker like the small boy thinks about all the bad things those kids are saying about him. "What a fatass, no wonder he was almost late to class." "Why is he even in Honors Biology, he's so stupid." Tears threaten the blue eyes, but he was used to this. Nobody loved him, because of who he was. So he would try hiding it from everybody. He'd try starving himself, but it was so hard not to eat. His weight was also a genetic thing, so it was harder to lose.

Another negative to his life is that he's questioning his sexuality. Who'd love a fat gay man? Who'd love a fat anything? Nobody. That's why he'd hide forever.

After high school our young Jonathan discovers YouTube. He posts some clips of him playing Call of Duty, multiplayer, ninja defusing bombs. He'd laugh at the launches of the dead bodies, sometimes his own, because he was too late to defuse the bomb.

Before in high school Jonathan said no one would love him, but years later on YouTube he's made friends and has millions of people who love him for who he is, because no one knows what he looks like, and they never would, because he's fat. He'd joke about girls' boobs a lot, and sometimes joke about sucking dick. Jonathan was bisexual, but still didn't want people to know. You never know what people will despise you of; weight, facial appearances, tattoos, piercings, sexuality, etc. Anything you're sensitive about in your real life shouldn't be known on social media... Hence the reason Jonathan, known as H2O Delirious online, because no one really knows his name, unless they watched his one Q & A years ago.

Delirious is very sensitive about his weight and sexuality. Speaking of, he checks his weight this morning for no apparent reason. Hint: The sarcasm in the narrator's voice. Every time he gets on to any of his social media he sees pictures of his friends and how... fit they are... and skinny.

In his bathroom he spots the truth telling monster in the corner of the room. He drags it out from the corner and stupidly puts it in front of the mirror. He's surprisingly wearing a t-shirt with the TARDIS on it from Doctor Who. Light lighting bolt shaped marks go across his upper arm, on both arms. He dislikes t-shirts, especially in public, but he stays at home most of the time.

Finally, he steps onto the machine. He wiggles his pallid toes and waits for the depressing truth. He looks down at the number, still able to see the number over his gut. He sighs, "285. Fuck." The clown frowns and steps off and pushes the machine away. He's balancing between 200 and 300, so fucking great, right? His friends joked he was merely 145 pounds, but were they wrong. He wishes he actually weighed that much.

The chubby raccoon plops into the computer chair of his and puts in his earbuds. He turns on his microphone. Skype pops up onto his desktop, and his friend from Canada appears onto his screen. "Hey Vanoss!" The clown is his perky self again, ignoring the situation that had happened just a few seconds ago. "How's life?" The owl questions, a smile plastered onto his face. "Wonderful, as per usual!" Delirious replies. He smiles back at his friend, even though he can't see him smiling. Dimples form onto the chubby face of his. His blue eyes sparkle as him and his friend continue chatting online, waiting for their other friends to show up for a round of Vespucci Job. Delirious was a little anxious, because he's never played this type of game on Grand Theft Auto yet.

On the other end of the Skype call Evan sits and stares at the black screen with the default face of a person with a perfectly circle head. Evan had no idea why his friend wouldn't at least show his face to his own friends. Sometimes it fluffed the owl's feathers, because CaRtOoNz knew what he looked like.

Jonathan did want to keep certain things private. Sort of how Evan tries keeping his musician life away from his gaming. Jonathan wanted to keep the way he looks away from people, Evan understood that, but what about his friends who were dying to see it?

"Do you know where everyone is? Why is it takin' so damn long?" Delirious questions and then chuckles. Evan looks up and shrugs, "I have no idea. If you want to we can chat later until they're actually ready?"

"Nah, it's okay. I don't mind chattin'," the raccoon answers. He looks down at his hotdog fingers, oblivious to the fact his answer just made his friend smile and blush.

"So, what'd you do this morning?" Evan questions, taking a bite of his cold pizza. Jonathan thinks back to the weight machine, "Uh, I just, uh…"

"What?" Evan leans onto the edge of his chair, awaiting his friend's answer. He hears his friend clear his throat. The owl has never heard this from his friend before; this quietness. Delirious was always good at starting conversations and keeping them going.

"You can tell me anything Delirious. I hope you know that," Evan tries to soothe his "quietness". Delirious sighs, "I can't really tell you, not yet." Why the fuck would you say that Delirious? Well… it's better than lying.

This answer makes Evan bite his lips and slowly nod, "Okay. It's okay." Evan didn't know asking a simple question would lead to an awkward conversation. He was now very curious as to what his friend did this morning, and why he really didn't want to talk about it. The Skype call grows quiet as each of them stare into the screen. Jonathan finally speaks up, "Vanoss… do you work out everyday?" He slightly regrets his question, but Evan still answers, "I mean, no, who the hell would want to do it everyday? I do it occasionally I guess. Why?"

"Just wonderin'. I was trying to… uh… open up my schedule to work out even more than I do now." Okay Jonathan, you can stop lying to your fucking friend now. "Oh, alright. Where do you work out at?"

"Planet Fitness. There's one at the shopping center I live nearby."

"Sweet," Evan says and laughs, "how much can you lift?"

The raccoon cracks his knuckles, "I could probably lift you up."

"Oh really?"

"Over my head."

"I'd like to see that happen," Evan teases. They both laugh for a while, "I'd love to see it happen," Jonathan states between laughs. An idea sprouts into the head of the owl's. What if he made a surprise visit?

Another face finally appears on the screen; Moo, and another one; Ohm. "You fuckboys ready to play?" Ohm shouts his question. "Hell yeah!" Delirious cheers, changing his emotion from before when he and Evan were chatting. Evan notices this as well, he wishes Delirious would open up to him more. For now the friends merely play games, laugh and yell at each other for content online. But the one question still floats around the owl's mind; Should he visit?

Multiple questions fill Jonathan's head; Should he tell Evan the truth? That he's fat and afraid of what his army will think.

Should the clown try starving himself?

Maybe he'd get a boyfriend if he was thin...

Maybe he'd actually show his face to the world...

***

PLEASE READ THIS PART!!

So this story might not go on, I just want to see how you guys will react to it. This story is very close to home for me, because I'm pretty fat and I'm afraid that's the reason I'll never get a girlfriend. Because "all" lesbians are thin and fit as fuck.

So I'm just putting Delirious in my shoes, sorta. Hell, maybe he already is, but who knows? Am I right?

Now, for now until at least Capture is finished, or if I get a hella good idea and you guys love this story, I'm not going to update this one.

I love you all! (Don't know if I say that enough)

- HoodiniClown

Tell Me Why

"Tell me why- ain't nothin' but a heartbreak-" "Queer," someone in the hallway suddenly shouts. The younger Jonathan takes off his headphones and looks around for the suspect. A boy with long blond hair walks past him, "Why do fat people always listen to gay music?" He scoffs and rides away on his shitty skateboard. Jonathan rolls his blue eyes and continues jamming out, this time to NSYNC. To this day Justin Timberlake is still his hero.

"Delirious! Delirious! If we get out of here alive will you kiss me?" Vanoss shouts as he runs away from the scary monster chasing him. "What?!" Ohm questions and then laughs. Delirious's face goes bright red, "Uh, what?" The clown has become very silent. They ignore it, just like every other little flirty comment the guys make to each other sometimes.

Suddenly Delirious is sprinting to the opening, "Fuck, fuck, fuck," he mumbles over and over again. He finally runs through the opening and laughs, "Yes! Yes! We made it! We fuckin' made it!" They made it, but Delirious can't physically kiss Vanoss. Suddenly Jonathan thinks of them actually kissing, that'd be absurd. Delirious is too ugly to kiss a pretty set of lips like that.

"So what's next?" The same owl questions. Delirious looks at his friend on the computer screen. He then looks at his clock and curses, "I actually have to go guys. See ya!" The clown quickly logs off of his computer and gets dressed for work. Yes, work. You'd think YouTube would do the job for him, but it unfortunately wasn't. Jonathan curses as he slips on his black pants. He slips on a white shirt and a black vest over it. He hates the way it looks on him, but he has to wear it, or else he'd lose the job.

He hops into his blue jeep and drives to work in a rush.

He disobeys some traffic laws.

Music is blaring in his jeep as he gets ready for the blow from his boss, because he's late; again. He's now 20 minutes late for his first shift. "Fuck it," the clown grumbles in his car and drives through the intersection, but he didn't do it just because he's late to work; other thoughts were in that delirious mind when he drives through that red traffic light. Suddenly, a huge truck horn is heard in the distance as Delirious's blue jeep turns into jello.

The red cased phone vibrates in the pocket of the one and only, CaRtOoNz. "Wait guys, I gotta phone call," he speaks to the few friends of his playing Rainbow Siege with him. He whips out the phone and slides the answer button.

"Hello?"

"Hi, is this Luke Patterson?"

"Yes, this is him. May I ask who's calling?"

"NC Medical. You're a first contact for Jonathan Dennis correct?"

"I guess, why? What's wrong?" Luke now stands up from his gaming chair and rubs his beard. The nurse heavily sighs, "Your friend has been in a serious car accident."

"I'm on my way," CaRtOoNz answers and sprints out of his home leaving his friends online.

"So what happened?" Luke asks the nurse at the front desk; breathless. She clears her throat and asks Luke to follow her.

"So ran through a traffic light and a 18 wheeler hit him. A truck vs. an 2004 jeep isn't a fair fight."

"Oh my god."

"Jonathan was knocked out as soon as the truck came into contact with the jeep. He has a major concussion; the doctor will explain that later."

Luke nods.

"He has been out of surgery for 15 minutes now."

"Really? Why was he in surgery?"

"To remove all the debri from his body. He was nearly impaled all the way through. His lucky to have survived this."

The brown eyes look to the nurse in understanding, "So, has he woken up at all since he was brought to the hospital?"

"No, I'm afraid not. I'm sorry. We called you, because maybe all he needs it a close friend with him." The nurse sadly smiles and gestures Luke to walk into the room of Jonathan's.

CaRtOoNz opens the door to his broken friend. The left side of his head was bruised, a long scar ran down his neck and probably even further down the poor man's body. Scars crawl all over his left arm, down until his elbow where a blue cast starts. Luke grabs his friend's hand, "What the fuck were you doing out there man?" He sits with Jonathan for the rest of the day, occasionally using the restroom and eating.

In the morning Luke wakes up to the ringing of his phone. The contact says Vanoss, "What the fuck? Oh…" He slides to accept the call.

"Hey Evan, what's up?"

"Holy fuck, you sound tired."

Luke laughs, "Yeah sorry about that, I'm-"

"You're what?"

"I'm at the hospital," Luke bites his lip, knowing Delirious doesn't like it when he tells the guys stuff about him without his consent.

"Why are you at the hospital?" Evan panics, something Luke has never heard before. Not a "panic in a video game" kinda thing, but a "holy shit someone's in danger" kind of panic.

"Evan, if I tell you, you can't tell anyone else. Especially the guys online. You also can't flip your shit about this."

"Just… tell me why."

"Fine, it's Delirious."

"WHAT?"

"Evan!" Luke whisper-yells into the phone.

"Sorry, sorry. Why? What happened? Is he okay? He's not dead is he-?"

"Evan, calm your titties boy. He's… not dead. He just has a major concussion and lots of stitches."

"Oh thank God-"

"But Evan, he hasn't woken up since he's gotten here."

"I'm going."

"What?"

"I'm coming down."

"What? To North Carolina? To Delirious?!"

"Yes! I want to make sure he's okay physically, and mentally. He kinda sounded different when we were talking like the second to last time we played together."

"What do you mean?" Luke wanders outside of Delirious's hospital room and into the hallway. Evan clears his throat over the phone and thinks back to their conversation before their game of GMOD, "Well, I asked him what he did earlier that morning and he just got really quiet and didn't say anything to me. Then he asked me if I worked out everyday."

Luke peeks in at Delirious and understands his questioning. The man didn't like the way he looked, how much he weighed, but he loved everyone no matter what; except himself.

"Evan, I know why he acted like that, but I think you coming down here without him knowing would make him worse, mentally."

"But, I'm one of his friends."

"I know that, he knows that, but..."

"What?"

"I really wish I could just tell you."

"Tell me what? CaRtOoNz?"

"Why he acts this way around most of the guys."

"Tell me why CaRtOoNz, or I'll figure it out myself."

"Evan, you'll only make it worse. I'm sorry."

The line goes quiet for a little bit before Vanoss finally speaks.

"I just... really want to see him."

"Evan...Evan just try calling him first. Once he's up of course."

"Trust me, he's going to have multiple voicemails on his phone." They both laugh at the owl's comment. Evan sighs over the phone once again, "Luke?"

"Yeah?"

"Could you at least talk to him about me coming down to see him?"

"I will."

"And Luke?"

"Yup?"

"Tell him I miss him and I hope he gets better real soon."

Luke smiles at this, "I will Evan."

"Thank you man. Bye."

"Bye." Luke hangs up and then smiles at the generous Evan. "If only the damn clown could realize that his weight doesn't matter."

Oh CaRtOoNz it's not that easy.

The bearded man returns to the room and sits with his friend once again.

"Evan called," Luke states out loud, hoping his friend could hear. CaRtOoNz knows that as soon as Delirious would hear those two words a goofy smile would crawl across his face.

***

"Evan Called"

The hot showers run in the locker room. Guys get fully naked without batting an eye. Poor 10th grade Jonathan waits his turn for the showers. He waits for them to be empty.

Finally right before the end of the period all the guys are out dicking around near the lockers. Jonathan turns on the shower and washes the sweat off of himself. Today in gym they played volleyball, which he was surprisingly half decent at. As Jonathan continues showering and replaying the awesome serves he had, a sudden whistling echoes throughout the showers. The blue eyes go wide on the chubby face of the teenager. Maybe one of the boys at the lockers was a really loud whistler; Jonathan only hoped. With a sudden urge, the young clown scopes out the showers, spotting another boy on the other side of the showers. The blue eyes watch the soapy water run down from his curly hair, down his dark back and down his- "OH MY GOD! JONATHAN DENNIS HAS A BONER!" A kid shouts and the kid showering looks at the plum teenager. Jonathan instantly covers himself. Another kid laughs, "YOU CAN BARELY SEE IT UNDER THAT GUT OF HIS!"

Jonathan grabs his towel and pushes through the dickbags of kids. He quickly gets dressed in the bathroom stall. He washes off his face and stares at himself in the mirror, "Why am I so ugly and... fat?"

"You're not," a soft voice says. Jonathan's heart beats in his pierced ears, it's the boy from the showers. His bright smile makes his green eyes look like emeralds.

That look, that boy, made Jonathan feel something he's never felt before; a deep feeling of want, nervousness, and love.

At nearly midnight Jonathan's eyes flutter open. His pallid hand moves to wake up his sleeping friend.

"Luke," the clown weakly tries to get his friend's attention. The bearded man finally gets the hint and wakes his ass up. He smiles at his friend and hugs him, "Fuck! I knew I'd see those silly blue eyes again!" Delirious weakly laughs and then frowns at CaRtOoNz's "I'mma fucking rant" stance.

"What?" Delirious tries to sound innocent, but he damn well knew why his friend is mad.

"Don't "what" me. What the fuck were you doing Delirious? You nearly got yourself killed."

"I know, but-"

"But what man?! I was so fucking worried when I got the call from the hospital! Then they told me you had a concussion, and some cuts from the glass," Luke throws his arms in the air as he rants. Delirious sighs at his friend, "I'm sorry that I worried you CaRtOoNz. I... my..." Delirious has trouble speaking, this is a side effect of a concussion, but really he didn't want to tell CaRtOoNz the multiple reasons he crashed.

"Delirious? Are you okay?" The bearded man comes into full vision in front of the clown. He slowly shakes his head and then stays quiet, so Luke changes the subject, "Evan called." Delirious bites his lips and the inside of his cheek; this is a sign that Delirious is about to cry. Before Luke can say or do anything, Jonathan breaks into tears. His face turning red as he sobs, he brings his scarred hands to his face. "Johnny? Jonathan? Are you alright?" Luke sits on the bed beside him and tries comforting him. The bearded tickles Jonathan's shoulder as his friend leans his head on it.

After a little bit, Jonathan finally settles his crying. He turns to Luke and rubs his eyes, "You know I hate how much I weigh CaRtOoNz. You know that's my biggest insecurity."

"Yes, I know."

"I... I was late for work, because I was playing a little longer with Vanoss and a few of the other boys. So I rushed and didn't drive very safely, and at that stop light Luke..." Jonathan sobs and gives a guilty look at his friend, "I kept thinking about my weight and how I'd never find someone to love me, because of it. I thought about getting fired from work, losing everything. I thought-"

"You need to stop thinking," Luke stops Delirious mid-explanation. Delirious slowly nods and starts to laugh, "You're right, but I can't when all my friends are fit as a fiddle."

"Who cares? And actually not all of them are," Luke argues, "but if your weight mattered so much to them, why would they be your friends?"

Delirious shrugs at his friend, his eyes still glistening with tears. He merely shakes his head and then waits for a doctor or a nurse to come in. To let him go.

A few moments later, Jonathan sighs, "So what'd Evan call about?"

Luke clears his throat, "He was super worried about you."

Jonathan's heart skips a beat; why? Evan was a friend, he deserves to be worried.

"Did anyone else call?" Jonathan questions and Luke shakes his head, "No, nobody except Evan."

Another skip.

"Alrighty, what'd he want?"

Luke gives his friend a faint smile, afraid of the raccoon's reaction.

"Oh god…" Delirious is suddenly peeved at his friend.

"He wants to visit you-" Delirious tries to interrupt CaRtOoNz, but Luke holds his hands up to stop Delirious from speaking. "Before you say anything… Evan's very worried about you Delirious. Mentally and physically."

"Physically?" The clown snaps; glowering.

"No! Stop that! Stop being so angry!" Luke snaps at his friend, "These people fucking care about you. I told Evan about your accident and he got super worried. He wants to come and see you, but you're too worried about you goddamn appearance when you're a steaming hot man! You can't see that, but everyone else can!"

"Everyone else calls me fat! I get rude comments all the time Luke! At work! In the fucking store! Everywhere!"

"Everywhere except at home, and on the internet," Luke states, a pleading smile on his face, "Please, give Vanoss a chance. This will be a big step for you Jon. Maybe Evan will be the one to show you that nobody cares about your weight or how you look." Jonathan's heart skips another beat at the thought of Vanoss being the one to change his world. He gives a petulant sigh, "I... I guess he can come." CaRtOoNz jumps up from the bed and cheers, "Evan will be so happy to hear this! I can see you trying to hide that damn smile you clown! You're a lil excited too!" Jonathan finally laughs with his friend thinking; maybe this won't be too bad, Evan is a close friend of his.

"Mr. Dennis?" A tall doctor marches into the room with a clipboard. Jonathan nods at the doctor. Luke notices his friend go tense. The doctor walks toward him with a stolid look on his face. He didn't seem worried, or happy for Jonathan's situation. "Is everything okay, Doc?" CaRtOoNz wonders. The doctor sighs once again, "Well, due to Jonathan's concussion we'll have to run some tests on him. Has he been talking to you okay?"

"Yeah, just a few stuttering words."

"Yeah, but that's a usual thing," Delirious adds on. The doctor nods, "Well then that's good, but there's a slight chance Jonathan that you won't be able to look at a screen for the next week or so."

"That's okay," Jonathan agrees and then gets up off the bed to start the tests with the doctor, but as soon as he gets up his head starts to spin and a pounding pain rumbles through his skull.

"Ouch! Ouch!" He yells as the doctor and Luke grab him by the arms. He plops onto the bed and holds his head.

"Maybe more than a week or so," the doctor says with a hint of sorrow in his voice. "I guess we'll need a wheelchair to get you to the testing rooms, okay?"

"Yeah, yeah," Delirious mumbles as the doctor walks out into the hallway and yells for a nurse. He turns to Luke and frowns, the pain gradually getting worse. Tears threaten the eyes of the 31 year old man. He shakedly sighs and leans his head onto Luke's shoulder. The bearded man wraps his arm around his bud and squeezes him close, "It'll be alright." As he comforts Jonathan he pulls out his phone and texts Vanoss;

"He needs you."

"Is he okay with me coming?"

"He's more than okay, but right now he's not okay without you."

"What? What happened?"

"He can't walk straight and his head is killing him. I think his concussion is worse than we thought."

"Oh god, I'll book a ticket right now then. I'll see you guys soon."

"Okay."

The texting ends as the doctor walks in with a nurse following behind him with a wheelchair. Jonathan slips into it and the nurse pushes him out of the room. The doctor solemnly smiles at Luke and shuts the door as they make their way to the concussion tests.

***

How Long?

This wasn't Jonathan's first concussion. In high school he thought he was so good at volleyball he actually tried out for the boys' team. Remarkably he made the team. He loved the sport, just not the guys on the team. It was a very small team, because boys' volleyball wasn't really big in their school district.

Jonathan acquired his first concussion in his life on the second away game of the season.

The school marched in like they were kings. Their school colors were red and gold. One of the other boys on Jonathan's team named Richard who was seldom kind to Jonathan, told him that, "This school has made it to the championships for 10 years in a row, and they've placed each time."

Jonathan was on the JV team, which was made up of 9th and 10th graders. Jonathan didn't try out until 10th grade.

"Okay! Team captains!" Jonathan and another kid named Haden were the team captains. Jonathan was only chosen because he had bomb ass serves. Haden loved hitting the ground and hitting other people with the ball; he was a 9th grader then.

The two kids walk up to the one referee and greet the other team's captains. The kids look at Jonathan darkly. After flipping the coin, Jonathan won the toss and called serving, so the other team had receive.

The ref blows the whistle; a sign for Jonathan to serve. He threw the ball up with one hand and smacked it with the other. The other team had no problem with bumping it, setting it, and spiking it back over. Jonathan surprisingly returned the ball; red marks left on his forearms.

Once they rotated a few times, Jonathan was upfront and now a middle row hitter. He was blocking and up close to the net, staring down another kid across the net from him. He had pretty blond hair and dark brown eyes. The kid smiled at him when he noticed Jonathan staring, but soon after, Jonathan knew he had messed up big time; the smile was fake.

"Ethan!" The setter on the other team shouted and the blond kid ran up and smashed the ball; right into Jonathan's face. The team cheered as Jonathan fell to the ground. The world was spinning, but he could still see that Ethan kid. He seemed to get closer to Jonathan, right up against the net and till this day, Delirious has sworn to God, that this kid whispered, "faggot", as the 15 year old Jonathan went unconscious.

He didn't go to school for a week, which wasn't a lot for the little concussion he had, but getting hit in the face with a Wilson volleyball was a different feel than getting smashed by an 18 wheeler.

Luke waits impatiently in the hospital room of Jonathan's. The clown had to take multiple tests; one for memory, one for damage, and one for eye sight. That's what Luke thought anyway.

The phone buzzes on the bearded man. It's probably Evan, he thinks as he takes out the phone. CaRtOoNz slides his thumb across his phone, "Hello?"

"Hey! I should be there early in the morning tomorrow. Like 3:00."

"Holy shit," Luke sighs, "Well, right now I'm the only one who can physically drive. Delirious's jeep is a ball now."

"Damn. I'm sorry. If you want I can get a rental car-"

"Nah, I'll pick you up."

"So you're going to leave Delirious?"

"Evan, will you calm the hell down? He's not your wife," Luke laughs, "Besides, he's surrounded by nurses and doctors trained in school for plenty of years for this. He'll be fine."

"Yeah. Sorry I tend to overreact sometimes," Evan gets quiet on the other line.

"Is Delirious in there with you now?"

"No, he's taking concussion tests right now," both the men sigh at Luke's answer.

"Well, the I'm about to board. Text me as soon as he's done testing. Please."

"Sure thing. Call me when you land, aight?"

The men agree to each other's requests and hang up.

At about 5:00 Delirious is returned to his room in a wheelchair; the doctor behind him and the nurse with a clipboard. Luke stands from the chair, clasping his hands together as he speaks, "So, what're the results?" CaRtOoNz turns to a frowning Delirious. The doctor clears his throat and pushes the red framed glasses further onto the bridge of his nose. "Well, Jonathan cannot drive until next year around this time, June 30; his license is suspended and his vision isn't as well as it used to be. We'll need you back for an eye examine after your concussion has cleared up. This accident may have permanently damaged your vision, you may need glasses or contacts," the doctor explains and then looks at both of the men, only getting a worried look from Luke. He sighs and continues, "He also cannot look at any electronic screens for the next month."

"What!?" Delirious finally speaks.

"I'm sorry, but if you want this concussion to disappear Jonathan you'll need to stay away from reading anything for the next month, or playing video games, even texting friends."

"That's bull-"

"Knock it off Jon," Luke snaps at his friend. Delirious crosses his arms like a fussy toddler.

"One more thing," the doctor says. Delirious's head snaps back and he lets out a loud and obnoxious sigh. Luke gives him a dirty look as the doctor continues, "He'll need some type of mechanism to help him balance himself. We recommend a wheelchair, or crutches, maybe even a cane." Luke's eyes go wide, "How long will he need to do this?"

"About two weeks, by then his balance should be better."

"Okay," Luke says with a deadpan look on his face. The doctor begins to walk out, "Oh, and Jonathan can go home today. You'll just need to keep an eye on him, and we'll supply you with whatever mechanism he needs to use," the doctor smiles and then shuts the door. Jonathan heavily sighs, "Fuck. I fucked up so bad Luke."

"Well, at least you'll have two nurses to help you by tomorrow morning."

"What?"

"Evan needs to be picked up early from the airport tomorrow morning," CaRtOoNz explains to his poor friend.

"So far that's the only highlight of my week," the sad clown sighs and rests his elbow on his knee and his head on his hand. His hand pushes his cheeks, making his eye look swollen. Luke cracks his knuckles and then sits back into his own waiting chair, "So, wanna get out of here for dinner?"

"Sure," Delirious says with no emotion. Luke sighs, "Okay. Well, what thing do you wanna use to get around?"

"Well I don't want to be a fat person in a wheelchair, people might mistake me for a pregnant lady," Jonathan gloomy jokes. Luke stands up and squeezes his friend, "I'm glad you're okay man." Jonathan wraps his arms around his bearded friend. "Watch the bruise," Jonathan whines as Luke apologizes over and over again. The clown laughs at his friend's panic. Luke notices this, "I'mma put a damn bruise on the other side of your damn face," he threatens. Delirious continues laughing. He slowly abates his laughing and sighs, "I guess I'll take a crutch." CaRtOoNz frowns, "What if Vanoss and I carried you around?" Delirious wheezes, "You'd need the whole gang to carry me." Luke smacks his arm in the friend, "If you keep this shit up you'll have two people hitting your arm, because Evan will hate hearing you talk about yourself like this."

"He'll understand when he sees me CaRtOoNz," the sad clown is back. Luke sighs, "I have a feeling he'll change your perspective on yourself."

"Like one of those cheesy fanfictions between us?" If only, Delirious quickly thought, but immediately removed that thought of him and Evan together from his mind.

Luke laughs, "Yes, totally. I better be at the damn wedding, now let's get you a crutch and food in our bellies."

The boys get out of the hospital and get some food, but during their tasks Delirious can't remove the sickening feeling in his stomach, along with the thought of; Vanoss is going to see what he looks like in under 12 hours.

***

Pickup

Jonathan figured out he was bisexual in the summer of his 8th grade year.

It was a rainy July afternoon and the boy surprisingly didn't want to play video games. He instead sits in the living room and watches the rain drip from the roof and onto the windows. He also watches trucks and car speed by his home. An orange truck eventually catches his blue eye. It pulls into the parking lot of the house beside Jonathan's. A red minivan following close behind it and pulling in as well.   The blue eyes peek around the frame of the screen door. A family of four gets out of the van. Two children hop out of the back of the vehicle. A girl and boy, both seemed to be around Jonathan's age. A tap on the shoulder scares the 14 year old. He turns around to his smiling mother, "Why don't you go help them unload stuff?" Jonathan slowly nods and throws a blue hood up. He sticks his pallid hands into his pockets and runs over to them in the pouring rain. The little girl spots him, her dirty blonde ponytail flipping as she turns her attention toward him. Her smiling green eyes greet him. She's really pretty, is all that fills the 14 year old's mind. Her smile makes his gut ache and his arms weak. "Hi! I'm Bella!" She sticks out a sun-kissed hand. Her nails are painted a baby blue. Jonathan notices, "I love your nail color." They both chuckle and instantly click. "I'm Jonathan by the way. I came over here to see if y'all needed any help." Bella beatifically shows Jonathan to the back of the truck. "You can help me take my dresser up to my room," she orders and Jonathan grabs a hold of the scratched up pink dresser. They walk off the truck and into the truck. Before they march up the stairs with the dresser, someone walks down. "Wait," Bella warns, "my brother is coming down." The blue eyes gaze at the tall brown-haired boy. His dark brown eyes lock with Jonathan's. He waves at him and smiles, killing Jonathan once again, just like his sister's smile. The boy makes it down the stairs and sticks his hand out to Delirious. A blue string bracelet hangs off of his wrist. Jonathan takes the hand. The boy smiles, "I'm Weston. I'm Bella's older brother."

"I'm Jonathan, nice to meet you," the young clown shakes his hand back. They let go, but seem to continue staring at each other. "What grade are you in Jonathan?" Weston questions his newly made acquaintance. He clears his throat, "I'm going into high school. I'll be a freshman."

"Hey so will I!" Bella steps in. Weston grins, "I'm going to be a sophomore, so we're all close in age. That's neat. Welp, I'll see you around Jonathan." Weston walks away to grab more of his stuff from the moving truck. Jonathan smiles at Bella and then they work their way up the steps with the dresser. As they push up the steps Jonathan thinks, he can't be gay. He doesn't like boys, but Weston made him feel all dreamingly inside. The darkness of his eyes and the little tips of his brown hair a lighter color due to being in the sun.

Jonathan found Bella to be attractive too, or was he just a desperate kid and liked anyone who came into his path? Hoping for them to like him back. Maybe he was desperate because he's fat. Maybe Jonathan just liked boys and girls. People do that right?

Later that night Jonathan asks his mother, "Can one person like boys and girls Mom?"

"Yes, sweetie. Why?"

"What's that called?"

"Bisexual, dear. Why?"

"Just curious," the boy answers and continues picking at his steak. He thought in his head while his fork poked into the meat; Jonathan Lee Dennis, bisexual.

Delirious stares out the window as CaRtOoNz pulls into the airport. The blue eyes look amazing in the purple sunrise. Luke turns and stares as well, his brown eyes turning a beautiful gold color. They wait for their friend to come through the glass doors. Luke dramatically sighs. Delirious rolls his eyes, "What?"

"Why the hell are you wearing that big ass sweater? It's the middle of July."

He doesn't answer.

"Delirious?"

"What?"

"Answer me, please."

The clown heavily sighs, "Why do you think I'm wearing it?"

"I asked you!" Luke starts to get a little petulant, "Delirious! You need to stop acting like a damn baby!"

"It's not my fault I'm fucking self conscious about my damn weight!"

The car immediately grows quiet as the two wait for Vanoss. Delirious obviously can't handle the quiet, so he turns up the radio. Joan Jett &

The Heartbreakers blares over the radio as the boys continue staring out of the windows. As Joan Jett sings, "I hate myself for lovin' you!" Mr. VanossGaming strolls out from the glass door and strides his way over to the car. The clown's heart nearly bursts and his face turns a bright red as he watches his friend throw his stuff in the back. Delirious quickly throws the hood up on the huge, gray hoodie of his. As the door opens and closes the heartbeat of the poor raccoon goes faster than a rabbit's. "Hey you guys," Vanoss greets his friends with a guttural voice. "Hey Evan!" Luke greets back. The bearded man turns to his hooded friend, waiting for him to respond. "Delirious, come the fuck on."

"Hey, Luke, it's okay. He doesn't have to show me his face. Yet," the owl teases.

"He should still say "hi" or some shit," he snaps and turns his head toward Delirious. The clown sighs, "Hey Vanoss."

"See, was it that damn hard?"

"Shut the fuck up Luke," the raccoon bites. Evan sits back into the seat and looks worriedly at the friends. They stay silent nearly the whole ride home, making their new coming guest uncomfortable.

Back at the house Jonathan rushes out of the car, clenching the gray hoodie closer to himself, along with his crutch. Vanoss rushes out of the car after him, but Luke grabs his arm, "Don't help him yet. He's not ready," Luke explains and Vanoss sighs. Evan grabs his bags and turns to Luke, "Is he alright at least?" CaRtOoNz sighs, "No. He's not. I need your help showing him that he is." They both carry in Vanoss's bags and set them into the guest room in Delirious's house. "There's a lot of neat stuff in here," the owl hoots while looking at his friend's action figures and different nerdy things.

Upstairs Jonathan plops into his bed and covers himself up. Snuggling up like a baby raccoon. He wishes he were a raccoon, so he wouldn't have to show Vanoss his face, or anyone. Plus raccoons are considered cute no matter their size.

The door peeks open and Delirious goes undercover. "It's just me you fuckin' baby," Luke petutlanty states. He sits on his friend's bed, "You're bein' a very bad guest to Evan. I hope you know that." Delirious groans and flips the blanket and hood off of his face. "At least show him your face."

"Why? So he could be disgusted?"

"Jonathan," Luke pulls out the first name. The clown groans and gets out of his bed. "You go first," he orders like a toddler. Luke rolls his eyes and marches out the door. He occasionally turns around to make sure Delirious is still behind him. They both go down the stairs and Delirious gets a terrible feeling in his stomach. With each step and sound of his metal clutch his heart beats hardly in his ears. He stumbles and grabs onto CaRtOoNz's back. What if the clown faked himself passing out? He did have a concussion, but him falling down the steps would be Vanoss's first impression of him; physically. The clown takes a deep breath and finally accepts the fact that Vanoss is going to see his face no matter what.

***

He's Not Alright

"Come on Johnny!" Mama Dennis shouts from the driveway at her 7 year old son. His two other siblings ride their bikes perfectly around him. The young blue eyes stare at the long street. Could he ride it without his training wheels? "You can do it Jon!" His older sister Jennifer tries to encourage him. "You got it bud!" The eldest of the three children, Samuel, shouts. "I'm too scared to Mom!" Jonathan shouts from the end of the driveway. "How do you know? You've never ridden without your training wheels boy!" His mother shouts back. Jonathan sighs, she's right. How could he know if he's never tried it? He was also surrounded by people he loves and trusts,; they'll be there to support him.

Only if the young clown thought about that now.

The little legs push off and survive on the bike perfectly. His family cheers behind him as he rides back and forth on their street. He smiles a bright smile as he calmly rides his bike back to his driveway; rocks popping under the bike from the pressure.

He did it! With his family by his side! For now on Jonathan was going to try things. New things.

Jonathan totally didn't try anything new. He couldn't even show one of his closest friends his face.

Evan stands down stairs and examines a few of Delirious's collectables. He hears the steps creaking and turns around to find CaRtOoNz. "Oh, Luke! How's Delirious-?" Evan immediately focuses on the person walking behind Luke. His piercing blue eyes glance at Evan and then turn away. His dark brown hair is noticeably played with his fingers. His head is shaved on both sides, except for the stuff on the middle of his hair. His eyes were the best to Evan, but what really killed the owl was the smile. The clown nervously smiles and adorable dimples pop out on both sides of his cheeks. He wanted to go up and squeeze the hell out of him.

Delirious does jazz hands, but Evan doesn't respond. Luke smiles, "Holy shit."

"What?" Jonathan questions and uncomfortably shifts his crutch.

Evan was still mesmerized by the looks of his friend. He didn't notice he was staring. He was taking in all the wonderful details of his face, but why?

"He's stunned. In a good way," Luke states and gestures toward their feathered friend. Jonathan stares into the brown eyes of his friend's; wondering why the hell he's staring. "Evan?" The first name of the younger man echoes in his head. Vanoss finally snaps when Delirious hits him with his crutch. He smiles, this killing the clown; pay back.

"You look amazing," Vanoss admits and doesn't realize what he's just said. Jonathan's heart melts. This is the total opposite of what he thought Evan was going to do, or say. The clown's face turns red, he stammers, "Th-thank you." The living room of the clown grows quiet, as the two continue staring at each other. "Anyway!" Luke comes in for the rescue, "Woo-hoo! Another friend knows what Delirious looks like. So how about breakfast?"

"Sure," Evan says dreamingly. Luke slaps him on the shoulder; really hard. Evan slowly turns to Luke and is faced with a straining smile. "Why don't you talk while I find us a place to eat?"

"No, Luke-!" CaRtOoNz is already walking away with his face in his phone; ignoring Delirious. They both sigh. Jonathan makes his way to the couch and Vanoss sits right down. He shamefully watches Delirious easily sit down. "How's your head?" The owl asks. Jonathan's head pounds at the question. "Well," he laughs, "it still hurts and I still get dizzy sometimes." Vanoss nods with a small frown on his face.

"So, do you mind me asking how you got into the crash?" Evan sits Indian-style on the couch, facing his friend. Jonathan bites his lip and twiddles his chubby thumbs; he's still wearing the big ass sweater. Should Jonathan tell Evan the truth? He could trust him right? They've known each other for a while now.

"I... fuck, Evan this is so much at once," Jonathan's voice was so soft. Vanoss has never heard the clown like this before. The friend scoots closer, "I'm here Delirious." The teary blue eyes meet the understanding brown ones. "Part of me wanted to crash Evan," his voice cracks and tears start to slide down his plump cheeks. Evan notices his face turning red. It must happen when he cries, the owl concludes. A tan hand wraps around the wrist of the pale clown. He squeezes until he can feel the wrist of his friend under the huge hoodie of his.

"I wanted to crash, because I hate myself. I hate the way I look and..." he inhales a jagged breath, "my weight," he nearly whispers. Evan squeezes his wrist. That's why he fucking asked you about exercise you dick, but what did he do that morning that he couldn't tell you about? The owl thinks deeply about his poor friend. Evan watches each tear slip from the soft blue eyes. He's not alright Evan, do something. "I'm sorry Delirious. I am, and personally, I don't give a fuck about weight. You look-"

"No shit you don't care. Look at you," Delirious sobs. He rubs his eyes with his pallid hands, making Evan's hand slip from his wrist. Vanoss frowns, he made it worse, he made it about himself. "Fuck, Delirious! I'm sorry!" Vanoss tries grabbing his wrist again, he's never touched anyone so comfortably before. "Delirious I fucked up, please stay sitting. You can't be walking around a lot anyway. You might fall over," Vanoss orders with a worried look. Jonathan stays, but doesn't talk or look at Evan. The two stay silent and wait for CaRtOoNz.

A sigh from the clown breaks the silence, "You said I look amazing. Is that true? Or were you just trying to make me feel better about myself, because Luke told you about my bullshit?" Jonathan has his arms crossed and a stern glare toward Vanoss. A petulant sigh is released from the owl, "Well, your face is amazing. Your dimples, your eyes, and God your smile. Your personality is what really ties it all together though. You're like a little gift, and that hoodie is a ribbon away from you expressing your body, and how you don't give a shit about what people think. You usually don't Delirious."

"You're right, but that's in video games and shit Vanoss. Real life isn't a damn video game, and if it were I'd recreate myself in the Sims and fix this shit."

Vanoss thinks, and finally asks, "what are you most worried about with your weight?"

Jonathan thinks, his blue eyes wandering to the ceiling fan in his living room. In the reflection of the one glass lamp he could see the figure of Evan in it. Delirious frowns and finally answers, "Getting a date. Never being able to find someone to love. Nobody loves fat people." Evan frowns and opens his mouth to say something that would have changed Jonathan's point of view on himself right then and there, but Evan bottled that feeling up and tucked it away somewhere. ***

The Waffle House

As a child Jonathan's father would always take them out for breakfast on Saturday mornings. This all ended when Jonathan turned 14 and figured out he was bisexual. He's heard his father's ramblings many times before about "the gays". Jonathan suddenly didn't feel safe around him anymore.

One Saturday morning in January, the Dennis children and their father went out on their usual breakfast to the Waffle House. Jonathan was in 10th grade, his only sister was in her freshman year of college and Samuel was on his way to becoming an architect, but somehow they were all still together and going out for breakfast with their father.

They sit at the small yellow table and wait to order their food. Jenny sits beside Jonathan across from Samuel and his father.

After ordering their food Mr. Dennis speaks up. "Why are y'all so quiet? What's going on in life?" None of the children say anything. Their father sighs, "Fine, how about we all go around and say something new? Hmm?" Jonathan sighs, he just wanted to stare out the window and watch the cars go by on the freeway while having the glorious smell of waffles and bacon shoved up his nose. Why couldn't the family accept each other's existence; wasn't that enough for love?

"Well, I'm passing all my classes," Jenny says without any emotion. She stares at Sam, gesturing that it is his turn to speak. "I'm starting my plans on my very first building," he finally speaks. Before Jonathan can announce his news, their waitress brings their breakfast. The 10th grader quickly thanks the Gods and Goddesses who timed this situation.

As they chow down Delirious's father speaks up once again, "So Johnny, anything new?" His chubby little hands grip a little tighter onto the fork. Cue in one of the "That's So Raven" visions as Jonathan remembers his recent "play date" with Weston. The two were hanging out in the bedroom of the 11th grader. Weston was showing Delirious the new video games he got for Christmas. One of those games being Silent Hill 2. Weston was too scared to explore the abandoned hospital so Delirious took control. All Weston stated was, "You're so brave," and the two made the mistake of making eye contact. Delirious ignored the zombie nurse limping over to him and he set the blue Dualshock controller down. Weston's hand was warm on Delirious's black painted nails; painted by Weston's sister. The teenagers push their lips together, but they don't pull away instantly. Weston closes his eyes and continues his hand up to Delirious's arm. The black tipped fingers play with the strings on the gray hoodie of his friend's. Weston finally pushes away and slowly opens his brown eyes, "I like you," he finally says; his lips trembling. "Why?" Is the first word that comes out of the young clown's soft lips. "I'm fat," he states and looks down at himself. The older boy grabs his chin, "That doesn't matter," Weston answers. They both smile. Weston was the one and only boy to say that to Delirious.

Back at the diner Jonathan smiles, "I'm dating someone." The whole family gasps, surprised that the younger boy had a girlfriend. Well, everyone was thinking girlfriend.

"Who is she?" Mr. Dennis immediately asks. Jonathan frowns and picks at his chocolate chipped waffle, "It's not a "she" Dad," he answers and sinks further down into his seat, trying to hide behind Jenny. The two other siblings turn to their father to see his reaction. His nose flairs and he takes another bite out of his omelette. He doesn't look at Jonathan for the rest of the meal, or the car ride home, but as soon as they returned home Jonathan got an ass whooping and was banned to ever hang out with any friends until his stupid phase was over.

Jokes on his dad, the boy he was dating was only a window away.

Plus it wasn't a phase.

"How's the Waffle House sound?" Luke questions, but his shoulders droop at the sight of Delirious obviously ignoring Vanoss. "What the fuck guys?" He throws his arms up, "Welp, I'll see y'all in the car." The front door slams. Delirious groans, "I hate the fucking Waffle House."

"Why?" Vanoss questions as he stands up off the couch. He waits for Delirious to get up, just in case him standing up makes him dizzy. The clown clears his throat, "I... I told my father something when we were eating breakfast there and he strongly disapproved." Multiple ideas of what Delirious told his father then went through Evan's head. One of them being that he was gay. Deep down Vanoss had only hoped, which was really stupid in the owl's logical part of his mind.

After watching him Vanoss fixes his denim jacket and follows Delirious out the door. The car seating is the same as it was merely an hour ago. Delirious messes with the radio trying to find a good song or good station. Woman Woman by AWOLNATION comes on and Jonathan gradually head bangs; harder and harder. He smiles, the music flowing through his veins. Evan easily jams in the back, tapping his foot. This was the type of music he liked and the kind he composed. Luke notices both of them jamming, but still not saying anything to each other, maybe Evan could help Luke help Jonathan; that is what Evan is here for.

At the Waffle House the boys order and chat while they wait. Luke starts up a deep conversation, "So, Delirious, how do you feel about dating?"

"Just because you're taking me out for breakfast doesn't mean I'll fall for you CaRtOoNz."

"Not like that you damn clown. I meant, like, what if Evan and I helped you set up a dating account on something to help you find someone."

"How will dating help?" The raccoon questions. Luke clears his throat and quickly looks at Evan and then back to Jon, "If someone finds you attractive and likes you for who you are, maybe it'll show you how to love yourself." Evan nods in agreement with his other friend, "He's right Delirious."

The food arrives, but the conversation continues, "So, what happened at the Waffle House many years ago Delirious? You told me you hated it," Evan questions while he bites down on a piece of bacon. Jonathan's heart pounds in his ears. He strongly grasps his fork and clear his throat, "Well Vanoss, as I said before, I told my father something and he didn't like it. That's all." Evan nods and respects his answer, but Luke pushes, "Wait, what? You never told me this."

"Fuck," Delirious throws his fork down and rests his head on his hands. Evan jumps at the sudden angry action. The owl watches the fork sink into the syrup on the clown's plate. "Jon-?"

"I told my dad I was datin' a fucking boy and how I was bisexual. Okay? We got home and he fucking lashed out on me! Okay? Y'all happy that you know? Huh? You both know why I hate the Waffle House and now Evan knows my sexual orientation. Merry fuckin' Christmas!" Jonathan stands up from the table, grabs his crutch and rushes to the bathroom, "I don't need to eat anyway, I'm big enough," he mumbles.

Evan slowly turns to CaRtOoNz. They both have worrisome looks on their faces. "Should we go after him?" Vanoss asks Luke. He shakes his head, "No, he'll come out eventually, we'll just have to wait."

They waited a very long time.

***

A Shoulder To Lean On

Jonathan's sister, Jenny, was there for him after he came out to his dad. After the Waffle House situation Jennifer would never leave her little brother's side. Sam would go back and forth. Sometimes he'd stand with Dad sometimes he'd stand with Jonathan. Jonathan's mother loved them no matter what; she didn't care what type music they liked, what they wanted to be when they were older, what gender they liked, etc. She loved them and only cared if they were happy or not. So that meant occasionally Mr and Mrs. Dennis would get into fights over certain things. Like when Jenny started dating a boy who was too "punk" for her, as their father stated. His name is Luke. Even after Jenny and Luke split Jonathan and Luke were still really good friends, even though Jonathan was still in high school while Luke was out of school.

One time Luke invited Jonathan to one of his DJ sessions. While Jonathan watched CaRtOoNz do his stuff he wondered if Luke was trustful enough for Jonathan to tell him about his sexuality. On Luke's break the 17 year old Delirious finally felt like it was time to tell his friend the deep secret of his. "I'm bisexual," he says quickly and tries to run from his friend. Luke sets down his drink, "Okay? Do you like me or somethin'?" He questioned, but Jonathan knew he was just joking. "I just felt like you should know,"

Jonathan embarrassingly admits. Luke laughs, "I don't really care dude. You're my friend no matter what gender ya like." They hug and Luke carries on with his session. Throughout their future years together Luke would try hooking Delirious with people, but he gradually realized that Jonathan didn't even like himself, so why would he like other people?

Luke continues to be the shoulder for Jonathan, but nowadays he needs two shoulders because he's a big baby.

"I thought you said he was going to come out?" Evan asks CaRtOoNz as they both pick at their food, both of them suddenly not hungry. "I thought so too, but I guess he's really hurt. Evan I don't know what the hell to do anymore," Luke complains and sets his fork down. Evan impatiently taps his foot and finally snaps, "Fuck it." He pushes his plate away from himself and marches to the bathroom. He nearly rips down the bathroom door. "Jonathan?" His real name feels so weird on the lips of the owl. He searches under the stalls for the familiar black Converse of Delirious's. He spots them in the last stall. "Jonathan, please come out."

No answer.

"Jonathan, I'm sorry I asked that question. I just really want to know more about you, so I can help. I'm really sorry."

Nothing.

"Delirious? Please! I'm sorry. Fuck. I fucked up again, alright?" The owl slides against the bathroom wall and waits for his friend. He thinks about how he's felt recently, maybe Evan could sympathize with the clown. "Hey, if it makes you feel any better... I," he twiddles his thumbs, "I'm... fuck... I haven't even said this out loud to myself yet." Evan breathes heavily, "I'm gay Jonathan."

The stall slowly opens to a red faced, semi-smirking clown. The blue eyes look down and connect to the brown ones. Evan stands up and wraps his arms around the raccoon. They both laugh at each other and then make their way back out to the car.

When they arrive home Luke announces, "I'm gonna go home for a little while. Please don't kill each other." Jonathan slowly gets out of the car, with Evan right behind him. "Alright, see ya," Delirious waves and makes his way to the house. Evan stays back and chats with Luke. The bearded man leans out the window, "Please take care of him Vanoss. I don't know what you said in that bathroom, but it worked. I've never seen him so... relieved? I don't know, but please don't fight or say anything stupid. Aight? Text me if you need anything." Vanoss nods and waves at CaRtOoNz as he backs out of the driveway. He walks into the house to spot Delirious on the couch. The clown stares at him like he's trying to finish a puzzle. "When did you figure out you were gay?" Evan sighs at Delirious's question. Evan thinks for a moment, "Well, at first I was so confused. So like a little after I released U-RITE, so like around the end of summer last year."

"Yeah," Delirious slowly nods. Vanoss continues, "Making music just gave me time to really think, ya know? And I slowly realized why I couldn't get a girlfriend for a while; it wasn't because I was busy with music and gaming, but because I didn't want to date a girl, and trust me, I tried my hardest to like a girl again, but instead whatever God or Goddess above was like, "Let's shove all the men possible into his life." So all I'd see were magazines with men posing on them, commercials with men, ads on social media, and then they made me develop a crush on a man."

"Do you still like them?" The clown questions and squeezes the pillow on the couch. Evan smiles, "Unfortunately, I do." Jonathan scoots closer to Evan, "So, who is it?" He asks like a teenage girl at a slumber party. "It doesn't matter right now. I'm kinda tired, are you?" Vanoss asks in a rush and pretends to yawn and stretch. He should have lied to Delirious, but why? He's never been this open with someone. Vanoss wants to tell him the truth, it's just that he and Luke are supposed to help Delirious find a date and what good would Vanoss do if he told him the truth. The truth would hold Jonathan back. Why? Because the truth is Vanoss's crush is on the man sitting right next to him.

***

Setting Up

J onathan didn't date after he and Weston broke up. He was really heartbroken. The only thing that helped him were video games and occasionally music.

"Jonathan, I think we should stop dating."

"Why do you think that Wes?" Jonathan intertwines his fingers with his boyfriend's.

"Because I'm leaving for college soon. We should think about our futures instead."

"But I see you in my future Weston. God please don't do this," Jonathan's voice cracks as tears form in his sad blue eyes. "Jonathan, I'm sorry," Weston pushes his hand away from Jonathan and asks him to leave. The clown goes home, runs up to his room avoiding any contact with his family. Jonathan promised himself something that day; he'd never date again.

Again, another promise of Jonathan broken. "So, which app do you wanna use? Since you prefer both," Evan questions as he looks at the app store on Delirious's phone. Delirious merely shrugs at the question. "Ask Luke. He's good with apps like that," he answers as he puts another dish away into the cupboard. Evan petulantly sighs, "This is for you Delirious! Not CaRtOoNz!" The clown shrugs once again. This action makes the feathers on the owl fluff, "Are you fucking kidding me? Why are you such a baby Delirious? Huh? What's the matter?" Jonathan stops putting the dishes away. He sets the rag up onto the counter, "I really don't want to go through the pain again Evan. The pain of someone leaving me. Someone being disgusted by me, because of my weight, and my appearance." Evan slams Delirious's phone down onto the couch and stands up violently, "There's nothing wrong with your appearance. You're hot!" The owl's face goes red after his little babble of words. He genuinely thinks his friend is attractive and his personality his amazing, but he needs to find someone better than this narcissistic Evan.

After lunch Luke arrives at Jonathan's house, "So how's the dating goin'? Did you help him Evan?" The owl frowns and shakes his head, "He's being a little stubborn." Luke heavily sighs and sets the bags of food on the coffee table, "So, where's he at right now?" He questions Evan. The Asian looks around, "I think he's playing on his computer." Another angry noise is released from the bearded man, "Delirious! Get your ass out here!"

A few moments later Jonathan strides out, "What?"

"Come here," Luke orders. Delirious sighs and plops down onto the couch beside Evan, "What do you want?"

"You need to fucking made up your mind. You're not just gonna sit in here for the rest of your life playin' video games! Evan and I here are gonna help you! We're trying to help you Jonathan! Can't you see!" Luke's voice cracks, and Evan whips his head around to him. He rubs his beard and sighs, "We both deeply care for you Delirious. Please cooperate," CaRtOoNz pleads and Vanoss's heart breaks; he agrees. "Delirious, please try. I know it sucks-"

"No you don't. You've never been fat Evan," Jonathan spats. Luke growls, "Stop using that fucking excuse boy! Your body size shouldn't fucking matter! If that date of your's can't see that, then they're not fucking worth it!"

"What about in bed then? Hmm? That's my biggest fuckin' fear CaRtOoNz. Who wants to have sex with a fat guy? Hmm? None of y'all would do it, would ya?"

"I would," Evan snaps back. Luke stares at the back of the owl's head. A quick silence falls over them, but Vanoss fixes it, "Anyway, sex shouldn't matter right now. When you get there, you get there," he explains. He smiles at Delirious. A smile the clown's never seen before. It made him feel warm, like after walking inside your house after playing in the snow for a while. He ignores that feeling and smiles, "Welp, let's get this dating thing on the road."

"Setting up this shit is hard," Luke groans as all three men surround the computer of Delirious's. Evan fixes his glasses as he looks at the options. "So, are we doing Grindr?" The owl questions the raccoon beside him. The blue eyes search the screen, "Yeah. Let's do that."

"Bisexual? Correct."

"Yes."

"Any preferences?"

"Fuck no. I'm not a racist piece of shit."

"Not what I meant, but that's good too."

"Bio?" Luke questions.

"Video games, music, long walks on the-"

"Don't Delirious," Evan laughs.

"Fine, what now?" Jonathan questions his two friends. Luke sighs, "Now a photo! Then we wait for any responses."

"I feel like fucking Paul Blart."

"But you're not a mall cop, and he's not bisexual, he's also not as young as you," Evan points out. Luke nods in agreement. "So, you're gonna wear your favorite hoodie?"

"Yeah. Is there something wrong with that?" The clown asks and looks at both of his friends. Luke looks at Evan and vice versa. "No," they answer at the same time.

"Smile!" CaRtOoNz shouts as he takes the picture of the smiling clown. Evan watches his teeth flash and his pierced ears move as he smiles. His blue eyes seem to glow to the owl. In fanfictions Vanoss has read he's usually obsessed with Delirious's eyes, but really he found his cheeks and ears the most alluring thing about him. His smile crushed every bone in the muscular body of Evan, because he knew he'd never have that man for himself. What could he say? The owl is falling out of his tree for this raccoon, but yet he's still helping him find someone to date.

The guys continue the rest of their day playing video games together on Delirious's Wii. Luke has never seen Delirious this happy in a while. "It's your turn to choose a song to dance to!" The bearded man shouts at the clown. "I can't dance in front of y'all," Jonathan pushes the offer away. Evan notices the coy smile. He stands and reaches at hand out for the raccoon, "Come on, I'll dance with you."

"Evan-"

"I hate dancing Delirious. I'm doing this for you," Vanoss explains and nervously laughs. "Fine," Jonathan smiles and takes his hand. They are currently playing Just Dance 2017. Jonathan scrolls through the different songs and picks the holy iconic song "What Is Love" by Haddaway. Evan laughs, "Oh fuck." The song starts out and the Delirious immediately gets into it. Evan's still a little nervous and slowly moves along. He turns to look at Jonathan dancing with a bright smile on his face. They both laugh at each other and continue dancing like there's no one around them. Luke laughs at them, but stops once he realizes how much they keep turning to each other. He thinks while he occasionally moves to the music. As the song ends they continue laughing, nearly out of breath. They smile at each other and CaRtOoNz notices something flash through Jonathan's blue eyes. A flash Luke remembers only seeing when Delirious was around Weston.

***

Match

<hr>

Jonathan was always a nervous person at first. He'd be very quiet and would always have his head down. He'd bite his lips and bounce his leg. When he was around Weston all of these things happened. Mainly at first when they would hang out every once and a while, but as soon as they both noticed signs that they liked each other all of these nervous habits disappeared.

"Hey Weston!"

"Jon! Hey!"

"You needed to talk to me?" The young boy rubs his arm as he awaits his crush's answer.

"Yeah, let's just play video games for now. I got a bunch for Christmas! There's this one called Silent Hill 2 you should try!"

"Aight let's go!" The boys make their way upstairs. Like it was explained before, that's when Delirious had his first kiss, but the conversation afterward was different.

Weston finally pushes away from the kiss and slowly opens his brown eyes, "I like you," he finally says; his lips trembling. "Why?" Is the first word that comes out of the young clown's soft lips. "I'm fat," he states and looks down at himself. The older boy grabs his chin, "That doesn't matter," Weston answers. They both smile. "I find you very attractive, plus you're funny and like a billion of other things."

A few nights later the boys lay on the roof right outside Weston's window. The younger boy lays on the stomach of the older one. Weston runs his fingers through the shaggy hair of his boyfriend, making Delirious smile and close his eyes in delight. "What do you wanna do?" Weston pretty much whispers. "I want to hear you explain to me why you'd ever like me," Jonathan demands and sits up on his elbows and turns to his boyfriend. Weston smiles, "Gladly." He then gestures for Delirious to lay onto his stomach again. "You're laugh," Weston gives a cheeky smile as he stares up at the stars. "The way your eyes sparkle when you're explaining a new video game to me. Everytime your face turns red when I flirt with you. Your soft lips. Your painted nails. The way you roll up your sleeves on your hoodie when you're getting pissed at a video game," Weston pauses and laughs. He feels Delirious chuckle as well. For the rest of the night they stay up and talk and occasionally make out.

Delirious loved Weston, but Weston didn't love him as much as he loved his career.

Early in the morning, Jonathan's phone vibrates and the light illuminates in his room. He groans and looks at the message. His eyes ache from the brightness. The clown reads the notification and jumps out of bed. He runs out of his room and bangs on the guest room door, "Evan! Evan! I got a match!"

Inside the room, Evan groans at Delirious. He's not mad that someone matched with Delirious, but he's not happy either. "Holy fuck! He wants to go out tonight!" Evan groans even more. He rolls over in bed and cuddles with his pillow. He slowly falls back asleep.

Delirious sneaks into Evan's room. He stops when he's realized that his friend has fallen asleep again. Jonathan stares at his sleeping posture and the way his face his mashed up against the pillow; like a sleeping toddler. A warm feeling consumes Jonathan as Evan rubs his face into the pillow even more. Suddenly the clown's phone vibrates. He looks down to see a message from CaRtOoNz saying, "What the fuck are you doing?" Jonathan snaps his head toward the door and shamefully walks out of the room.

Luke grabs Delirious by the shoulders, "Where you just watching Evan sleep?"

"No," he lies straight through his teeth. CaRtOoNz sighs, "If you like him Delirious you should probably stop the whole Grindr thing."

"I don't like him. He'd never like me back anyway," the raccoon frowns, but then perks up again, "I got a match!"

"What?! Who? When?"

"Tonight! And his username is silentwestern. He plays video games and loves music. He also lives around here, and has grown up in the same town as me in North Carolina. Isn't that neat?" Luke looks a little curious, "Can I see a picture of him?" Delirious shows him the picture of a man with tan skin, dark brown eyes and platinum blond hair, like it was just bleached. He also has a septum piercing.

"Neat," CaRtOoNz states and looks at Delirious and he notices something, "Why the hell ain't you using your crutch?"

"Well, I was so excited, plus I'm getting better, obviously. I can use my phone without getting a headache."

"And you can see every word clearly?" Delirious looks down at his phone and just like a magic word Luke said, the clown suddenly couldn't read the words. His head started pounding. "Ouch, my head..." Jonathan stumbles backwards. Luke grabs him before he falls down the steps. He gives him a warning glance, like a mother looking at her daughter before going on a date with some new dude, "Do you really think you can go on a date tonight?"

"I want to Luke," the raccoon whines. Luke frowns, "I know you do, but you physically can't."

"What if I'm better by tonight Luke? Please." CaRtOoNz stares at the pleading Delirious. He tries his best not to look into his puppy dog eyes. "Fine, but I'm going to text your boy about your current conditions," Luke demand. A sigh is released, followed by a, "Okay."

Later on the guys sit in the dining room of Delirious's, they chat about how tonight might go. "So, are you guys gonna help me pick out my clothing?" Jonathan questions. Evan takes another mouth full of Chinese food and looks to Luke for an answer. Luke takes a swig of his soda and smiles, "Welp, I'm sure Evan wouldn't mind helpin' ya." Vanoss nearly chokes on the piece of chicken in his rice. "Yeah," he chokes out and takes a drink of his water. Jonathan nods at him and continues eating. "You should help too," Jonathan recommends to his other friend. "Actually, Luke you should help me find clothes and then Evan and judge." Everyone silently agrees to Delirious's terms. Evan wouldn't mind checking out Delirious for fun.

***

Do you guys need me to italicize Jonathan's memories so you know when it switches back to reality?

"You Always Look Hot!"

"Jonathan sweetie, why don't you go to prom with Weston?" His mother questions as she sets down his basket of folded clothes. Jonathan sighs, "Because I'd have to dress up. There's no suit that'd fit me right." His mother heavily sighs and warmly smiles. She makes her way over to Jonathan and sits at the edge of his bed. She grabs his hand, "We can find a tux for you Johnny. I promise." The blue eyes look up into his mother's warm sky colored eyes, "Thanks Mom." Jonathan goes in for a hug. As soon as they pull away his mother asks, "So, did Weston ask yet? Or did you?"

"No," Jonathan looks down at his hands and starts picking at his nail polish. A mischievous smile is placed on his mother's lips, "What if I helped you ask him?"

"Mom!" Jonathan lightly punches his mom in the arm.

"Oh come on! I could come up with some cheesy question!"

The two bicker back and forth for the night, but eventually agree to come up with a way to ask Weston to prom.

"I'll find you something Delirious!" Luke shouts from the closet. The clown sits in the bathroom in his underwear. He sighs thinking he'll never find a good outfit for tonight. He'll never find someone to love him. Jonathan is suddenly standing in front of the bathroom mirror. He seems to be having a staring contest with himself. His hands travel by themselves. His index finger travels over the light purple lighting bolts on his stomach. The pallid hands grab the gut and squeeze it; wishing it'd all just disappear. How could he ever have sex with this thing covering his dick? Jonathan thinks back to the shower situation in school. Why'd he ever remember it? Why'd he like boys? Why'd he like girls? Why was he fat? Why was he alive... A knock on the door scares Delirious. "It's Luke! I think I got the perfect outfit." Jonathan opens the door just enough to grab the clothing. He examines the different pieces of clothing his friend has picked out for him. A gray button-up dress shirt. A white undershirt just incase, and black jean shorts. The door opens again quickly. Jonathan whips around, nearly getting whiplash, and spots black Vans on the floor in front of the door. He shyly smiles and starts to put on the clothing. The jeans fit perfectly; they end right above his knee. Curse his Italian heritage for giving him dark hair on his legs. He quietly chuckles at his thought. He slips on the under shirt and then puts on the button-up. He prays as he buttons each button, hoping the next button will actually button.

Delirious nearly cries when he sees himself in the mirror. He looked half decent. He slips on his shoes and peeks out the bathroom door. He turns back and looks in the bathroom, like he's missing something. He looks down at his hand on the doorknob. His unpainted nails catch his atten-tion. He hasn't painted his nails since... Weston. The clown immediately rejects that idea.

"Are y'all ready!?" Delirious shouts down the stairs. Both of the guys shout a "yes!" Evan's heart gradually gets heavier in his ears as he listens to each footstep down the stairs. Just like in every movie or T.V show ever were the girl is going to a dance for her first time, Delirious walks down the stairs in slow motion. Luke's eyes go wide and his jaw drops. Evan's face goes red and his body goes numb. Jonathan stops at the end of the stairs and does a few poses, "So? How is it?" Evan stammers before actually talking, "Luke did a very good job. Holy shit. You look hot. I mean you always look hot! But this is a ten times better than a hoodie and jeans dude." CaRtOoNz looks at Evan weirdly, he said "hot" a lot in that sentence; to Delirious. Friends do that to each other though, so maybe he's just being nice. It'd be fucking perfect though if Vanoss had feelings for Jonathan. God, did CaRtOoNz hit the nail on the head.

"Delirious, I do have one recommendation," Vanoss stands up off the couch. Jonathan puts his hands on his hips, "What is that, sir?"

"Eyeliner," he demands.

"Really?"

"Yeah. It'd make your eyes pop even more than they already do," Evan explains and once again Luke takes that as a "friendly" saying.

Delirious starts up the stairs back to the bathroom, but stops halfway up the steps, "Oh, by the way, my date will be here in a half an hour!" Evan snaps his head back to Luke. "He's coming here, Luke?!"

"Yeah. Is that a problem, Evan?" The bearded man questions the flustered owl. The owl doesn't answer. Luke sighs, "Is there something you need to say or do Evan?" The brown eyes slowly turn to the bearded man, "I think... I think I do... I need help CaRtOoNz."

"Now damnit, you came here to help Delirious. Not to get help," Luke states and chuckles. Evan groans and rolls his eyes, "Please Luke."

"Fine."

"I think we should wait until Delirious is gone though."

"Why?"

"Because... it's... it's a... It's about him Luke," Evan finally spats out. CaRtOoNz nods, he has an idea of what it could be. Before he can say anything else to Evan, the doorbell rings. The two give a look of horror to each other. Evan runs to the kitchen and Luke quickly gets up to the door. He peeks through the little peephole and nearly faints at the sight. The color washes from his face, even from his damn beard. "Oh fuck. No wonder he looked familiar," he whispers to himself. Delirious is going to piss out of his eyes if he figures out who his date is. Or he'll be super happy and lovestruck, but goddammit, the kid broke it off with him, because of his career. CaRtOoNz sighs, "Delirious! Your date is here!"

The clown rushes down the stairs like a mexican jumping bean. Luke has never seen him like this. Delirious nods at Luke and opens the door and his jaw drops. Mixed emotions go across both of their faces.

"Jonathan?"

"Weston?"

***

Reunited

"**J**onathan! Weston's here!" Jenny shouts as Weston walks through the front door with a rose and a dark tux with an orange bow tie. Upstairs the young clown's nerves race. He smiles at himself in the mirror and walks out of his room.

Downstairs everyone waits for the young Delirious. Everything seems to be in slow motion picture. Weston's dark eyes gazingly stare at his prom date. His soft brown hair glows in the living room light, along with his blue eyes. The brown eyes move down to the midnight blue suit on the junior. Down the sleeves to the pale, black finger-painted nails. The dark nails crawl down the railing of the stairs. Blue eyes meet brown and both hearts melt. "You look dashing," the older boy complements. Jonathan's face goes red, "Thank you. You look amazing as well. I can't believe we're going together."

"I'm super glad we are. I wouldn't want to spend my last prom with anyone else," Weston smiles and grabs Jonathan's hand. He hands the flower to his boyfriend and he smells it, a smile crawling across his face. "Are you ready?" Weston asks his date with a warming smile. The clown nods, dimples appearing with the smile attached. After a few pictures, the teenagers finally leave for prom.

The night was wonderful for Jonathan. He's never felt so much love before; and it was genuine! That's what he thought though. A few weeks when summer would arrive Weston would break the poor boy's heart.

The men continue staring at each other, no words, no movements, just dropped jaws and strong eye contact. Luke looks at the both of them, "Are y'all alright?" The brown eyes search both pairs of eyes. He rubs his beard and shrugs, "Welp, good luck Delirious, hope y'all have fun!" CaRtOoNz pushes Delirious out and slams the door. He heavily sighs and walks into the kitchen for the hidden owl.

Jonathan's mouth moves, but no words come out. Weston tries moving his hands, but again, nothing. "Fuck," finally comes out of the clown's mouth. Mixed feelings were flying through him, like multiple ghosts trying to possess him at once; angry, happy, ashamed, humorous, morose, etc. Weston watches these multiple expressions go over his date's face. "What's wrong?" He chokes out. Delirious whips his head around, "What's wrong?! You left me years ago and now... now you're back!" Weston frowns and steps back from the angry raccoon. "You're still mad?"

"Still mad? You broke my fucking heart Wes! I thought you were the one for me! I planned our fuckin' wedding! How many children or pets we'd have together!" Delirious admits in a rush and immediately regrets it. "I'm sorry Weston. Wanna go to dinner and talk about it?"

"Hell yes, and I'm sorry too," he solemnly smiles. Jonathan shares the same smile and suddenly has the urge to kiss him, but for now he links his arm with Weston's and the walk to his car.

"Where's your car?" The date questions. Jonathan sighs, "I'll explain later."

"What'd you need to talk to me about, Evan?" CaRtOoNz pours a glass of whiskey for both men. Evan sits at the counter like a sad guy at a bar after a break-up. Vanoss grabs the whiskey and takes a small swig from it. He slams it down on the counter, "I think I like Delirious." Luke nearly drops the whole damn bottle of alcohol on the floor. He still slams it on the counter aggressively, "You fuckin' what?!" Evan suddenly starts sobbing like a damn baby, "I... I like Delirious!" He groans and rests his head on the cold counter top. Luke sighs and rubs his friend's shoulder, "Why didn't you tell him?" The owl pops out from his arm nest, "Because we were making him a date. I don't wanna ruin that," he sarcastically states the last part. "You shoulda told him before he accepted Weston's date."

"Weston? You know his name?"

"Oh God Evan. You're gonna hate this part," Luke sadly smiles at the lovestruck Vanoss.

"I was so worried about tonight," Delirious admits to his date. Weston smiled understandingly, "You're still handsome. No matter your size. Speaking of, you look a lil thinner."

Jonathan scoffs, "Oh, a "lil"? Fuckin' thanks."

"You're still a crabby little bitch aren't you?" The platinum blond comments. Delirious rolls his eyes and sips on his soda. He stares at Weston as he looks out the window toward the street. His eyes glisten in the small light at the pizzeria.

The lack of conversation kills the raccoon. He looks for something to talk about. Finally, he spots his date's nose, "What made you get the septum piercing?"

"You honestly," he smirks, making Jon's face go red. "Wh...what?"

"After getting my company up I just thought about you all the time."

"Why? I thought your career was more than me?"

"My career is you Johnny."

"What the fuck do you mean? What the hell even is your company?"

"It's clothing for plus-size men."

"No fucking way..." Jonathan nearly passes out. He didn't know if he's angry or happy for him.

"So why the hell is Delirious on a date with this guy if he broke his heart?" Evan questions before finishing his third glass of whiskey. Luke puts away the drink before the owl goes overboard, "Well, we'll figure that out when he gets back."

Evan sighs, "You know that saying, or whatever the hell it is?" He hiccups and then continues, "like, if you get back with your childhood boyfriend or girlfriend, like, it lasts forever?" A pained look goes across Vanoss's face. CaRtOoNz frowns. He thinks of a way to make him feel better, "I don't think he will. Evan you should tell him tomorrow morning."

"What? But what if his date went well? I don't to fuck stuff up for him!"

"Don't you want him to be with you, Evan?"

"Yes," he hiccups, "but I also want him to be happy."

Delirious picks at his stromboli, "A fucking plus-size clothing line for men? That's fucking awesome?"

"It's not just for grown men Jon. It's for younger boys too."

"Like that store, Torrid, for women."

"Yeah," Weston agrees and takes a bite out of his slice of pizza, "I was wondering if you'd want to be a model for it?" Jonathan immediately stops eating, "What? I mean... I've got work... ya know... I play video games for a living!" Weston tilts his head, "For a living? Are you a steamer or-?

"YouTuber."

"Oh, what's your name?"

"You can't tell anyone fuckin' jack Wes, only if I tell you."

"I promise," Weston holds out his pinkie finger. The blue eyes roll, but the finger still connects.

"H2O Delirious."

"No way! I've watched him before! I love the guys you play with!" Weston jokes, "Especially that Vanoss guy! Y'all seem close!"

Vanoss... Jonathan thinks and shyly smiles at his date, "Yeah. We are. He's actually staying at my house to help me." Weston sets down his fork and his eyebrows furrow, "To help with what?"

"Uh..." the flustered raccoon panics, "Okay... so I got into an accident."

"How should I tell him CaRtOoNz?" Evan moans like a teenage girl. "I don't fuckin' know. Just say it!"

"But," Evan sobs and somehow acquired another cup of whiskey, "I'm too nervous!"

"Oh my fuckin' God dude. Honestly I think he likes you too," the bearded man finally admits. The owl instantly perks up, "What? Really?!"

"Yes, there's this look in his eyes he used to get around that fuck boy, Weston. While y'all were dancing I saw him look at you with the look in his eyes!"

"No way!" Evan cheered, again like a little girl.

"Why'd you do it on purpose?" Weston's brown eyes glisten with tears for Jonathan. The clown rubs the tears from his eyes, "Because, I fuckin' hated myself. I occasionally still do."

"Is that what Evan's there for? Is he supposed to help you feel better about yourself?" Delirious's face goes warm to Weston's askings.

"You're so hot!"

"I'd fuck you! Come on now!"

"Your size doesn't fucking matter!"

Jonathan gasps and tries hiding his face of realization. That's bad; he shouldn't be thinking about someone else while on a date.

Later on outside of Jonathan's house the two ex-boyfriends stand in front of each other. "Well, thanks Weston," Delirious finally speaks. The pale hand reaches for the doorknob but is stopped by a warm hand on his wrist. He turns around and Weston pushes him against the front door.

Evan drunkenly walks to the front window to see all the ruckus. He almost pulls down the curtain for support. The brown eyes search outside. He spots Delirious and that Weston prick making out. His current glass of whiskey slips from his hand and he falls off of the couch. The owl then smashes into the coffee table of Jonathan's.

Delirious shoves Weston away from him. A look of pain flashes through the oh-so familiar brown eyes that he does miss kissing each night under the stars. Jonathan groans and pulls him in for another kiss. Then he shoves him away, "Good night Weston."

Luke runs from the kitchen when Delirious shouts. "What?! What is it Jon-?" CaRtOoNz stops and stares at Delirious trying to stop blood from Evan's forearm. He's using napkins from the uninjured table.

Luke sweeps up the broken glass and tries soaking up the whiskey from the carpet. While doing this he watches Jonathan pick up Evan bridal style and carry him up the stairs. He must be hell of a lot better if he's able to carry another grown man up the steps. Luke sighs and continues scrubbing the floor.

Batcoon places BatOwl in bed and tucks him in. He sneaks downstairs to grab medication he'll need for the headache in the morning, plus the pain from his wounded arm. Delirious slowly closes the door, staring at Evan the whole time. Once the door is shut the clown starts to make his way downstairs. Suddenly his head starts pounding and his vision gets blurry. He clings onto the railing of the steps and shouts for CaRtOoNz.

"For fucks sake, boy, we're taking you to the doctor."

***

Decision

"Jonathan Lee Dennis! Get out of your room this instant!" Mother Dennis shouts and bangs on the door of her 8th grade son. "Come on baby! I'mma break this damn door down!" Jonathan hasn't left his room in two days. His mother was devastated; he missed multiple meals and probably hasn't showered yet. "Johnny please!" She shook the door-knob, but it didn't work. She went into full on mother mode and broke the door open to her son's room. The sight was terrible. "Oh no! Jennifer! Call the hospital! Please!" His mother laid him in her lap. She rubbed his soft brown hair as they waited for an ambulance. "Oh baby, why?" She stared at her unconscious son.

Later on at the hospital the doctors explained to Jonathan's mother that he didn't have enough nutrients and passed out from the lack of them.

Jonathan wasn't mad about passing out.

He was mad because he didn't look any different after starving himself.

The same doctor as before frowns at his patient, "We'll have to run more tests Mr. Dennis. I'm sorry."

"It's alright. If it's going to help me get better. I'll do as many tests as I can," Delirious states.

After the doctor leaves for a bit Jonathan decides to brew up a conversation with Luke, "So, what happened with Evan last night?" Luke sighs like he just watched a dog get shot, "He... he got drunk, because he was sad..." he honestly answers. Jonathan frowns, "What? Why was he sad?" Luke bites his lips; Evan's not gonna fucking do it. "Because you went on a date," CaRtOoNz admits in a rush. The eyebrows furrow on the patient, "Why would he be sad I went on a... oh. Does he...?" The clown suddenly goes quiet from nervousness. Luke then nods to Delirious's question, "Very much." Jonathan nearly screams. He was stuck between two men now. What the hell is he supposed to do without breaking someone's heart?

Well Weston did break your heart, get him back!

Yeah! Evan's a sweetheart!

But Jonathan doesn't fight fire with fire.

Who gives a shit! Evan's the one! Evan cares more!

Jonathan smiles as he realizes his new decision. The blue eyes slowly find the brown eyes of his friend. "What?" The bearded man questions. Delirious smiles, "I think I like Evan."

"More than Weston?"

"Yes!" Delirious answers and his heart beats loud in his ears. His cheeks turn a bright red and his eyes sparkle. Just like a miracle a nurse comes in, "You've got a visitor Mr. Dennis." It's gonna be Vanoss! That dream crashes when Weston appears with a handful of roses and a sideways smile plastered on his face.

His head pounds as he makes his way down the steps. He looks around for Delirious or CaRtOoNz, but neither of them seem to be around. Evan sighs and rubs his head as he makes his way to the kitchen for a glass of water. A note on the counter catches his eyes. He grabs it and starts scanning the scribbled words of Luke:Hey Evan! Hope you made up from your drinking yesterday! You passed out and cut your arm open on the coffee table. Delirious wrapped you up and carried you up to bed. I had to take him to the hospital, because his head is starting to act up again. You're more than welcome to come and visit! I'm pretty sure Delirious would want you to! ;) - Your's Truly, CaRtOoNzEvan smiles at the parts about Jonathan. A warm feeling spreads through his body like jam. The feeling turns cold when he remembers why he passed out last night. He vaguely remembers seeing Delirious and Weston... making out. Vanoss groans and tears threaten his brown eyes. He shakingly sighs and shakes his head, "I'm such a fucking drama queen." He laughs and wipes his tears away. Maybe it'd be best for him to stay away from Delirious for a while. He should go back to Canada and stay out of contact until he gets over his stupid crush on the clown. The owl searches on his phone for the earliest train ride back to Toronto. Before going to pack he writes a note to his friends:I did make up! Thanks Delirious! I actually need to go back to Canada for a little while. So, I'm getting on a train that's leaving at 5:00. I'll try and visit again! Thanks for having me, and I hope you get better Delirious! Text me! Both of you! :)- The OwlP.S I hope you and Weston last forever...Evan sniffs and runs upstairs for his stuff.

"Okay Mr. Dennis! Your tests are back! And we know the problem. It's not permanent, but you'll need glasses until we call you back for another check up, alright?"

"Oh...okay?" Jonathan turns to Luke and then back at the doctor. He didn't make any contact at all with Weston. Except for when he hugged him and grabbed the flowers. Jonathan had his mind made up; he wants to be with Evan.

"So, for now you'll wait until your eye doctor calls you in to pick frames and they'll re-test you for the prescription you'll need," the doctor explains and starts to walk out, but he stops, "You can leave by the way." Jonathan whips his attention toward Luke and he nearly jumps out of the bed. They rush home to check on Evan. Weston decides to tag along.

Delirious is the first to barge in, "Vanoss?! We're home!" Luke runs upstairs to check. Delirious heavily sighs and looks everywhere downstairs. Weston tags behind. While they search in the bathroom downstairs, Weston decides it's a good idea to talk about last night, "So, are we gonna go on another date? I mean, that kiss was like a "yes" in my book." Jonathan turns to Weston, agitation burns in his blood, "No, Weston, we will not go on another date."

"But I love you Jonathan Dennis."

Jonathan scoffs, "You're such a big fat liar!" Before Weston can react, Luke runs down the stairs. Delirious jogs out of the bathroom, "Was he upstairs?"

"No! All of his stuff is gone too!"

Every bone and feeling seems to shatter in Delirious, "What?!" Luke frantically looks for any other clue downstairs. He runs back to his note he left Evan and finds the note from the owl. He reads it quickly and gasps. Jonathan speeds up beside him, "What is it?"

"He's getting on a train at 5 for Toronto!"

Adrenaline rushes through the clown as he runs out to Luke's care; oblivious to his concussion. "Come on! We need to go get him! I need to get him!" Delirious finally says and Weston final-fucking-ly gets the hint that

Jonathan has chosen Vanoss. The man runs off and doesn't look back. His heart is just as broken as Jonathan's was all those years ago.

Luke starts up his truck and looks at the time. "It's 4:00! We need to fuckin' book it to get to Evan in time!" Jonathan digs his nails into his thighs, "Then let's book it. I'm not letting him go. Even if it kills me." ***

The Owl

Jonathan always loved movies and TV, especially as he got older and more LGBT movies came to be. One night the 24-year-old was watching a movie and realized how in every gay romance movie he's watched, the actors have been super fit or thin. The young man has always tried looking past it. Just because it was in the movies doesn't mean that's the only way you can fall in love.

Size doesn't matter in any kind of relationship.

Evan knew that too.

CaRtOoNz slams on the breaks outside of the train station. Jonathan immediately jumps out of the tall truck and starts running toward the station. People are boarding the train. The blue eyes search over the multiple people; trying to find his friend. He looks for the jet black hair. The red duffle bag he brought with him, but he couldn't find him. He must be on the train already. Jonathan runs up to the conductor. The man stops him from getting on the train. "Please! My friend is on there! I need to talk to him!" The conductor sighs, "I'm sorry. Do you have a ticket?" Delirious groans, "No! Please! Can you at least get him?"

The conductor whispers to his co-worker. The other conductor walks back through the train. "Is there anyone on here named Evan?" He asks, and with Jonathan's luck, the owl has his earbuds in and sad music blaring through them as he stares out the window. So, he can't hear them asking for his name. The Good Side by Troye Sivan is playing as the train starts to move. The 26-year-old sighs as his mind plays fantasies of Delirious ever choosing him of his childhood lover.

"I'm sorry. No one answered, sir."

CaRtOoNz finally catches up to Delirious. Only in time for the train to start moving away. The clown wants to break down right there, but he wasn't going to. Suddenly the raccoon starts running with the train as it picks up speed. "Evan!" He shouts with so much pain in his voice. Delirious continues running and ignores Luke's shouts for him. The man is going to kill himself from running.

A few teenagers on the train start laughing in the seat in front of Evan. He pulls out one earbud to listen. "Hah! Look at that fat guy chase after the train!" Vanoss turns in his seat to look out the window. He spots the guy in a blue hoodie running. The blue hoodie. Evan meets those loving blue eyes once again. The heart melts on the asian man. He doesn't know what to do. Maybe he can get off at the next stop and go back for him. Evan presses his hands against the window. The train now goes too fast for Delirious. The brown eyes flash in worry as his friend falls to the ground. "Stop the train!" He shouts and people start looking around. They all stare at the red jacket wearing man. He grabs his stuff; fuck it. The tan hands pull on the red cord for emergency stop. The train slows to a stop and people groan and yell at Evan. An old couple watches Evan jump off the train and run down the track.

Vanoss grabs Delirious and pulls him up. The head pounds on the poor raccoon. Tears form in the corner of the brown eyes. Blue eyes meet those teary brown ones. They look at each other before Jonathan smashes his lips into Evan's. Vanoss drops his bag and holds onto the soft face. As Evan holds his face, Jonathan wraps his arm around his lower back and nearly picks him up. Just like in their call Jonathan said he could lift Evan, and look, he did.

The old couple turn to each other. The woman smiles at her husband and kisses him. The owl and the raccoon spread the love to the people on the train. Two girls on their way to New York share a kiss. A couple with a baby on the way smile and kiss each other. It was like a Hallmark original movie.

From a distance Luke watches his friends make out. He smiles and starts shaking his head, "I knew you had it in you Evan." The train starts moving again. Luke watches the two figures in the distance and notices one of them fall over. Like a voice in the wind he could hear Vanoss yell for help. By instinct, Luke starts to sprint toward his fallen friend. He arrives to a crying Vanoss and an unconscious Delirious.

Two men wait impatiently for their friend or new found love interest. Evan's legs continuously bounce up and down in anxiety. Luke watches the laces on his sneakers bounce up and down. He wonders if he should ask Vanoss about the kiss, but now probably wasn't the time. The wait another hour. Luke's stomach growls and he turns to ask Evan about getting food, but the man has fallen asleep. He sighs and just goes down the road to a drive thru, fast food joint.

In the drive thru to Mickey D's Luke nearly dies when he spots Weston in one of the windows. "Fuck," the bearded man grumbles and quickly grabs a hat from the back of the driver's seat.

Once it's Luke's turn to grab his food he pulls his hat down and takes the food without making any eye contact. In the window Weston tries figuring out who was in the big vehicle and why they were trying to hide. "Are you okay sir?" Luke sighs and makes his voice deeper, "Yes, thank you." Suddenly Weston starts laughing, "Luke! What are ya doin' hiding man?"

"I tried avoiding you," he gives in and takes off the hat.

"Why?" Weston asks, offended. CaRtOoNz groans, "I thought you'd want to talk to me about Delirious, so I tried avoiding you." Weston nods and then his face lights up, "Did you guys find Evan?"

"Yeah. We did. Jon did."

"I knew it. I'm glad he did," Weston's voice is suddenly poisonous. The window slams shut and Luke drives back to the hospital.

At the hospital CaRtOoNz picks at his fries waiting for a nurse or Evan to wake up. Like a genie grants his wish, Evan's eyes slowly open. "What smells good?" He looks around and spots the McDonalds bag sitting beside Luke. CaRtOoNz hands him his own bad, "I don't know what you like, but there you go."

"Thanks Luke," Evan tiredly mumbles and then starts eating fries. While chowing down, Luke decides to start a conversation, "How are you doing?"

"I mean, good, but... I don't know. So much happened at once," Vanoss explains and opens a box of chicken nuggets. Luke nods and takes the hint that Evan didn't want to talk right now.

A nurse finally walks out and asks for the family of Jonathan Dennis. Both Evan and Luke stand up. Evan pulls the at the sleeve of his own jacket, nervousness setting into both men as they follow the nurse. While they walk back the nurse explains to them that he's still unconscious, but the doctor will explain to them why.

Luke goes into the room first and frowns at his best friend. "I'm tired of seeing him like this," Luke admits out loud to Evan. The owl himself looks shaken up. "Why does he keep ending up in the hospital?" Vanoss questions. Luke shrugs with a frown still plastered on his face. "He keeps ending up in the hospital because he's not taking care of himself," a voice answers from behind. Both Luke and Evan whip around to be greeted by the doctor. "What do you mean he's not taking care of himself?" Luke asks, but he knows what the doctor means. The doctor sighs and looks over his glasses at the boys, "Jonathan is unconscious because he hasn't eaten in... from what we've gathered, about three days." Vanoss and CaRtOoNz turn to each other with a look of horror. "There's no way! He was just on a date yesterday. They must've eaten somethin'!" Luke argues with the doctor. "I'm sorry, but it's true. He passed out because he was using energy that wasn't even there. You seem to be a close friend for him Luke. I'm sorry to say this, but you guys need to treat him like a child and make sure he eats," the doctor explains. The doctor leaves the room in a gloomy mood.

Jonathan's been in and out of the hospital twice in one day, but it was worth it.

He found his owl.

***

Special Guest

Jonathan thought he fell in love with Weston. He was so kind to him and loved him for who he was and not for what he looked like. Weston did like the way Jonathan looked though.

When Jonathan was in the hospital after not eating meals he was miserable. Both of them were. Weston had no idea where Jonathan or his family went that morning. He was worried sick.

Jonathan stayed in the hospital overnight to rest and recover from his lack of nutrients. He made a big mistake, that didn't even work. His mother kept telling him how, "If you go from not eating at all to eating again you'll gain the weight faster than before." He also remembers his mother telling him how his weight was a genetic thing meaning it was more of a struggle to lose. On his father's side their metabolism was the worst thing. His father was on the bigger side like he. Jonathan's mother is curvy, but that's after having three children. Samuel was the smallest out of the three. He was tall and thin, but chubby in the face. Jennifer was a little overweight with some curves, but she's smaller than Jonathan and she's older than him. Jonathan always wanted a flat stomach, a thigh gap, thin arms, and no fucking back fat. The child needed to know that nobody is perfect and that he's fine the way he is.

The next morning when the young Delirious was in the hospital a special guest came in to see him. Weston held his hand as he stared at his sleeping crush, because at the time they had only known each other for two months, but they connected instantly.

Jonathan loved Weston…

And Weston couldn't handle Jonathan not loving him anymore.

But Jonathan wanted Evan.

"When do you think he's going to wake up?" Vanoss questions his bearded friend. Luke gives him a worried look, "I have no idea, but hopefully soon." They both turn to their sleeping friend. Evan's legs bounce up and down again in nervousness. CaRtOoNz sighs, it echoes in the quiet room of Jonathan's. He looks a Evan and notices how he stares at Delirious. His body posture is slouched, and usually he's sitting straight up and perky. His eyes seemed to be glued onto the man. "You love him don't you?" Luke's voice makes Vanoss jump in his seat. He shifts uncomfortably and looks at him weirdly, "What?"

"I see the way you're fuckin' staring at him like he's going to wake up any damn minute. You're worried for him. Hell, more worried than I am. You care for him deeply. You love him Evan, don't you?" Evan looks at his fingers and cracks them one by one. He sighs and places his hands in his lap. His sad brown eyes look to the sleeping Delirious. "For years we've teased each other, we've teased our subscribers about our relationship. I learn that he's in pain, mentally and physically, and I rush down here for him. I finally see his wonderful face, and realize he's ten times better in person, then he fucking chases down my train and kisses me in front of multiple people… Yes I fucking love him." A sly smirk comes across the bearded man's face. He watches the redness from Evan's face slowly disappear.

Luke eventually nods off into a deep sleep. Vanoss still sits and watches his sleeping friend. He ignores the yawn and the grogginess in his eyes. Without waking CaRtOoNz up, he scoots his chair closer to the bed. Once he sits in the chair he slowly and easily places his head onto Jonathan's soft chest. The tan hand slides down the bed and his fingers trace over the pale hands of Delirious. Eventually Evan falls asleep listening to Delirious's breathing and the heart monitor along with it.

Sweat drips off the forehead of the 10th grader as the whistle echoes in the gym. The blue eyes follow the ball as he throws it into the air and hits it over the net. When the ball gets to the other team, they disappear. The ball drops and bounces away on the other side of the court. The child looks around and notices his team is gone too. The crowd is gone. He's the only one in the gym; or so he thought. The ball disappears and the lights go out and quickly flick back on. Different spotlights turn on. One in front of him catches his young eyes. "Weston!" The young brown-haired, sun-kissed, boy stands with the ball in his hands and smiles, "Looking for this?" Jonathan starts to walk toward the ball, but then another spotlight appears a few feet beside Weston. An asian boy with very shaggy, black hair stands with another ball. He laughs and the voice sounds familiar, but two tones down from the grown man Jonathan knew. "Evan?" He gives a cheeky smile and throws and catches the ball, "Come and get it!" he teases. "Where am I? Why do I have to choose?" Jonathan panics and both children disappear.

Again Evan and Weston appear, but they're both adults. Evan throws the ball up and bumps the ball to Weston. Weston sets it and Evan spikes it into Weston's face. The both turn to Jonathan; who is also grown into an adult. "Are you going to choose Jonathan?" They ask in sync. Their sneakers squeak against the gym floor of Jonathan's high school. "Why do I have to choose? Something bad is going to happen to one of you. What am I choosing for?"

"Who do you love, Delirious?" Evan questions as he sets the volleyball in the air to Weston. He returns the spike into Evan's forearms. "Oh, I know!" The two other men suddenly disappear once again and Jonathan is left in darkness.

Little spotlights again shine on two grown men; Evan and Weston. "Hit the ball to whoever you choose to love Johnny," Weston purrs and gives a smug look to Evan. Jonathan knew who he was going to choose.

All of a sudden a volleyball bounces in front of him. He grabs the ball and bounces it himself a few times. He takes a deep breathe and looks at Weston. "I'm sorry," he states before setting the ball over to Evan. The lights flicker on and off again.

Jonathan is now passing the ball back and forth with Evan. Jonathan laughs as Evan hits the ground trying to get a low ball. As the asian chases after the ball Jonathan notices a person watching in the bleachers. His hair is a platinum blond, and from a distance it looks like he has a piercing in his nose. In the gym lights his face is glistening with tears. Evan notices Delirious staring and questions him, "Who's that?" Jonathan turns back to Vanoss, "I have no idea."

Jonathan's eyes slowly flutter open and adjust to the bright lights of his current environment. He goes to shift in his bed, but realizes there's something on him. The last thing he remembers is kissing Evan and... falling to the ground. His hand is warm, why is it warm? The blue eyes travel down and notices another hand on his. His gaze moves up the red sleeve of the leather jacket and to a sleeping owl. A smile appears across the pale face of the clown and his other hand rubs the weirdly soft hair of Vanoss. "I wonder what conditioner he uses," he wonders out loud. A loud noise scares him. It sounds like someone trying not to laugh, but laughing through their nostrils. He knew only one man who laughs like that. "Luke?"

"Did you really just ask yourself what kinda shampoo does Vanoss use?" His friend holds his gut as he laughs. "I hate you CaRtOoNz," Delirious spats, only to make him laugh even harder. The laughing makes Evan shift on Jonathan's chest, "Shh! You're going to wake him up!" Jonathan whisper-yells at Luke. "I'm sorry," he whispers back and calms himself down. The two stay silent until a nurse pops into the room, "I'm glad you're awake Mr. Dennis!" She cheers and immediately regrets it once she spots Evan, "Sorry," she whispers and continues, "You have a special guest here to see you. After he leaves we'll check your vitals and such. Then the doctor will explain what happened and what to do next, okay?" Jonathan felt a little uneasy, "Shouldn't he do that before I see someone?"

"Yes, but he's busy right now. One guest shouldn't hurt," the nurse reassures Jonathan. The nurse walks out of the room and gestures inside, "He's in here, sweetie." When the guest walks into the room Luke stands up like a bodyguard. "Weston?! What the fuck are you doing here?" Jonathan panics; this is the guy he saw in his dream! He has no idea who he is. Delirious squeezes Evan's hand to wake him up. Weston frowns at this action. He tries to act like he didn't see it, or that it cut him deeply, "How are you feeling Jonathan?" Evan glares at Weston, "What the hell are you doing here? He doesn't want you here!" Jonathan grabs onto Vanoss's upper arm and pulls him close. The monitor of Delirious's starts to get faster as he gradually panics more. "What's wrong Delirious?" Vanoss questions and places his hand on top of Jonathan's hand on his arm. Breathing gets faster and faster. Sweat starts to slide down his face. "Jonathan, are you okay?"

"No! No! I'm not! I don't know who he is!" Jonathan screams and everyone in the room gasps and turns to Weston. Tears don't hesitate to pour out of the brown eyes that were with Jonathan in high school. The eyes that loved staring into those blue eyes. Those light brown eyes were now replaced with darker brown eyes.

***

Forgotten

"Evan! Your uncles are here!" Mrs. Fong shouted from the bottom of the wooden stairs. The little Evan would peek his head out from his bedroom and come rushing down the stairs to greet his mother's brother and brother-in-law. Evan was merely 12 and had no idea his uncles were considered "different". He loved them for who they were. Every time his uncles visited, his father would go in to his study to "work". That didn't help Evan when he was 25 years old and questioning himself. He knew his mother wouldn't care, but his father definitely would make a big deal out of it.

Evan remembers the best of his uncles. Sometimes he wanted a relationship like them. They'd do everything together. Their laughs always sounded glorious together. Their hands fit perfectly together. They were two totally different people, but they loved each other for their wonderful personalities. Ever since Evan mentioned wanting to have a relationship like his uncles his father demanded for them to never come back to this house until Evan went off to college. He hasn't seen them since.

To this day his father of course doesn't know about his new found sexuality, plus the man just figured it out himself.

But now he has a boyfriend to show them as well.

Right now isn't about Evan though.

Weston throws the flowers on the ground and runs out of the room. Vanoss's hands stays attached to Delirious's hand as he sobs. Luke falls into his chair and lets out a sigh, "Holy shit. That's one way to get rid of him Delirious." Evan slowly turns to CaRtOoNz with a confused look, "I don't think he was trying to get rid of him. Well, maybe he was, but that's because... he doesn't know him."

"For real?"

"Yes."

"Stop fucking talking about me like I'm not here!" Jonathan shouts from the bed and squeezes Evan's hand. Suddenly, a nurse walks in from all the yelling, "Is everything alright?" Her sky blue eyes meet with all of the men's. Her eyes fall on Luke's worried face as he gestures towards the hallway. They walk out together as Delirious continues crying. Evan rubs his knuckles and it seems to calm him down. "Are you okay?" The owl questions with genuine concern. His warm thumb traces circles around the cold knuckles of the poor clown. "No, I'm not. Some random guy just came into our room and I just..." he trails off and squeezes his eyes shut as more tears slide down his face. Evan doesn't know if he should tell Jonathan that Weston wasn't a random guy, before he passed out. He didn't want him to freak out or to get extremely angry at him. "Jonathan... you knew that guy," Vanoss explains and clears his throat from tears. The sky blue eyes meet his with a look of confusion, "I did? Who was he to me Vanoss?" Evan sighs and clicks his tongue, "He was... your ex. You guys dated in high school. Then you went on another date, but then you realized you liked me and we-"

"We kissed," he finishes his sentence in a sweet voice. His pale hand finds its way to Evan's face. Jonathan decides to tell Evan about his dream, "When I was asleep I had a weird dream and in the end I had to choose you or that Weston guy. I chose you Evan," he explains. Evan's free hand removes Jonathan's hand from his face and their fingers hug together.

Out in the hallway Luke explains Jonathan's situation to the nurse. His hands move fiercely as he talks, "This one guy he used to know, well date in high school, came back into his life and they went on a date two nights ago, but he chose the guy sitting in there with him now. Anyway, he doesn't remember the guy who just stormed out. What's happening to him? I hope that's the only thing he forgets."

"Hopefully, but no one should be forgotten," the nurse speaks truthfully. Luke nods in agreement with her, "but then again he broke his heart in high school."

"Whatever, we need to run tests on him immediately," the nurse speaks demandingly and pushes Luke out of the way.

"We need to run tests Mr. Dennis. Just to be sure you won't lose anymore of your memory, okay?" Jonathan slightly turns to Luke and then to Evan with a look of bewilderment. He slightly nods and the nurse clears her throat, "So that means you two should go home and get rest. These tests may take a while." Evan groans, but eventually he and and CaRtOoNz leave the hospital. In the car ride home Evan brews up a chat with Luke, "I just want him to get better," he states out of the blue. Traffic and street lights shine in the brown eyes of both men. The older man rubs his beard, "Well, I'm pretty sure everyone would." He can hear the gulp in Evan's throat, "I mean like... I want him to look himself in the mirror and call himself attractive, because he is," he explains. Luke takes a glance at him, "and it's your job to get him to do that." Evan scoffs, "Why does he need someone else to show him that he's perfect the way he is?" The car grows quiet for a bit; only the soft music of Luke's plays. "I'm not leaving his side after this. I want him to get better. I want him to genuinely be happy," the owl states and the man beside him smiles with the brightest feeling inside of him.

The same doctor walks into Jonathan's room with a frown on his face. "Hey Mr. Dennis, how ya feeling?"

"Good-"

"That's a lie, obviously," the doctor cuts him off and sits at the edge of his bed. He cracks his knuckles and sighs, "Jonathan you've been in the hospital several times this month." Delirious slowly nods, "Yeah."

"That's bad, plus I noticed the reasons why you've been in the hospital," the doctor sighs once again and scribbles something down on his clipboard. He rips off the piece of paper and hands it to his patient. He's hesitant, but Jonathan eventually grabs it, "What's this?"

"A therapist."

***

Heyo, band camp is over! I can write again, but I got this idea from band camp, so another story should be up soon! It's a surprise I'm super excited about and I hope you guys are too!

Therapist

"I'm not getting him a damn therapist!" Jonathan's father shouts at his wife. The 14 year old hides in his room; waiting for the fight to blow over.

"Why in the hell shouldn't we? He needs help and we obviously aren't doing enough!" Tears stream out of the young blue eyes. He curls into himself as he listens to his parents fight over him. Why was he like this? He was so pathetic!

"Maybe you guys should give him a choice!" Jonathan's head peeks out of his black hood to the new voice in the fight. "It's his own mind, he needs to figure out himself if he needs this or not. You know you guys fighting isn't helping him either," Jennifer explains and a soft smile forms on Jonathan's lips. Later that day Jonathan chose not to go to a therapist.

This time he doesn't have a choice.

Jonathan needed professional help.

"He recommended a therapist?" Luke questions Delirious over the phone; on speaker so Evan could hear him too. "Yes, well more like a "you really need professional help" kinda recommend," Jonathan explains, his voice sounding just like it did on discord over a microphone. "Are you going to go to this therapist?" Evan now pops in with a question. The phone goes silent for a split second. "I have no idea honestly," the clown answers. "I think you should," Luke states to his friend. "Evan and I aren't really helping you. I mean you've been in the hospital multiple fucking times-"

"But that wasn't because of you guys. I'm just a fucking baby. I really need to straighten up. I'm starting to realize a few things in life anyway, and that's because of you Evan," Jonathan interrupts Luke. "Well, what if I helped you realize more things. When do you get out of the hospital?" Vanoss asks and turns to Luke. Delirious softly chuckles, "Come and get me."

Evan jogs up the stairs to get himself changed and to pick out clothing for Delirious to wear for their first date. He digs through his dresser and finds multiple clothes that he's never seen the man wear before. There's a reason though, a stupid reason; society. Evan sighs as the certain whiff of his new found love. His hands squeeze the clothing and he sits in his own thoughts for a bit. He's going to show Delirious he's the best fucking person in the world; in Evan's world anyway.

While Evan is upstairs, Luke decides to give Jonathan another call. He sits on the couch while the phone rings. "Hello? Luke? What's up?"

"Are you serious about what you said?"

"When?"

"Earlier, when we were chatting with Evan. You said you were starting to realize things in life."

"Yes, I was serious. Why wouldn't I be?"

"Because, I fucking know you dude. You're super good at pretending to be happy," Luke spats over the phone. He lowers his voice again to be sure Evan can't hear him. "So, Evan is making you genuinely happy?"

"Fuck yes he is! I haven't been this happy since…" Delirious cuts out and his mind goes blank.

"Weston?"

"Y…yeah?"

"You mean you sorta remember him? The blond guy with the nose piercing?"

"I know we dated and he was the first and only guy I've ever dated…" Luke shifts uncomfortably, "You fucking remember Weston?!"

"Yes! Yes! I sorta do! Okay!"

"When'd you figure this out?"

"I don't know, it just came back to me," Delirious explains, worry thick in his voice. Luke sighs, "Can you really just remember somethin' like that?"

"Something like what?" Evan questions as he walks down the stairs in ripped black skinny jeans, a white Metallica shirt, and black vans. On his back is a black bookbag with Jonathan's clothing and a special surprise in it for him. Something Evan found in his room while looking for clothes. Luke takes a fake smile across his face, "Delirious will explain to you later!"

"What was that about?" Evan questions in the car. Luke seems to drive faster and the music seems to be louder. "You're ignoring me Luke. What the hell happened? Is Delirious okay?"

"Just let him explain!"

"Why can't you?!"

Luke throws his hands into the air, "Fine! But you can't fucking hate on me or Delirious."

"Okay, why would I anyway?"

Luke heavily sighs and seems to have a staring contest with the road, "Well, Delirious sorta remembers who Weston is." CaRtOoNz leans closer to the car door, just in case Evan blows up. The truck is quiet for a bit as Vanoss gathers his thoughts. "Well, that's good then. His memory is strong. It was only short term!" Vanoss states and tries his damndest to hide the slight irritation in his gut. Delirious chose you, not Weston...

"So, do you really think Jon should get a therapist?" Evan asks Luke as they wait at a stoplight. CaRtOoNz taps his fingers on the steering wheel, "I think he already has one." A smirk crawls under the beard and the dark brown meets dark brown. "Me?" Vanoss's voice almost peaks. Luke laughs through his nose, trying not to laugh out loud. He fails and Evan joins in with the laughter. After the laughing fit and parking in the hospital parking lot, Luke grabs Evan's shoulder, "I really think if you weren't here right now, Delirious wouldn't be. You're his therapist Evan. You're his hero." A genuine smile goes across the younger man's face. He wraps his arms around Luke and then they hop out of the truck to great their recovering friend.

*** Short chapter, sorry, but y'all should be used to that...

Date

<hr>

Delirious doesn't remember his first date with Weston. He merely remembers them dating, just nothing in between. His memory is still jacked up from the train incident. This is a plus for his current love interest; Evan Fong, who is planning a date with the first man ever in his life.

"We're here for Jonathan Dennis!" Evan explains in a rush and the nurse gestures for the two to go back. The heart seems to pound in the ears of the young man as they arrive to his room. Luke slowly pushes the door open and smiles at the nurse. The blue eyes seem to thirst for the dark brown ones. They've just seen each other yesterday, why did they miss each other so much? Is it because of what Delirious said? The fact that Evan is helping him realize different things in life. For one, everyone can be loved, no matter what.

Evan's sneakers squeak on the floor as he enters the room. He chuckles to himself as he locks eyes with Jonathan. "I brought you clothes," he explains and sets the bag on the chair. "I... uh ... also found something in your bedroom when I was looking for your clothing." A confused look crawls across the clown's face, "What is it?" Evan unzips the front pocket of the bag and pulls out a fluffy animal. Vanoss brings the bear to him and the blue eyes seem to stare into the bear's. "You found Ted," Jonathan exclaims and rubs the bear's belly with his thumb. "Thank you Evan. Here, I'll get changed." As the nurse takes all the medical stuff off of Delirious, Luke makes his way over to Vanoss. Once Jonathan is in the bathroom, CaRtOoNz freaks out on Evan, "YOU TOUCHED HIS TEDDY AND HE DIDN'T FLIP OUT! THAT'S BULL SHIT! HE THREATENS TO KILL ME IF I LOOK AT IT! FUCK!" Luke whisper-yells and spits all over Evan's face. He curses and wipes off his face. "Maybe I'm special," Evan teasingly states.

In the bathroom Jonathan takes out all of his clothing and sets them on the bathroom sink. He goes from head to toe, examining what Vanoss picked out for him. A soft blue t-shirt and a pair of black basketball shorts. He doesn't like showing his arms and legs in public, but Evan would be there with him, plus Evan didn't know about every little thing Jonathan hates.

He undoes the hospital gown and throws it over the toilet seat. The warm shower water feels wonderful on his back. He hasn't seen his naked body in a while. Water drips from his brown hair as he stares down at his belly. "What's Evan see in this?" He mumbles, water droplets fall from his lips as he speaks. In Jonathan's head it was like Shrek and Fiona. Jonathan being the ugly ogre and Evan being the beautiful princess. He sighs and continues his depressing shower; he doesn't want to keep the beautiful princess waiting.

"Hey I'll need your truck," Evan randomly states toward CaRtOoNz. He whips around, "Why?"

"Because, I need it for our date. I can call you an Uber," Evan offers with a mysterious smile. Luke sighs, "Only because I love Delirious and y'all are fucking cute- BUT WAIT! NO NASTY IN MY BABY PLEASE!" Evan's face goes as red as the jacket on his GTA character. The owl slowly nods and catches the keys from Luke. As he shoves them into his pocket the door creaks open and both men snap their necks towards their friend. Evan takes in the looks from his date. He can't help the smile that forms across his lips. The scar on his neck from the car crash seems to have faded a little bit. Down his arm he sees the little scars from the debri. "Do I look alright?" He squeaks out and Evan nearly melts. "Yes, you look wonderful," he states as blush goes across both their faces. Luke rolls his eyes at the two dorks. "Welp, you two have fun. Stay together, be careful, use protect-" Jonathan punches Luke in the arm. He yelps in pain and steps back, chuckling.

As they walk out of the hospital the hands of the two brush together every once and awhile. Butterflies flutter in Jonathan's stomach and warm waves flood through Evan's body. In the back Luke shouts, "Just hold fuckin' hands!" They turn around and glare at him. After turning around they both seem to casually try and hold hands. At first they both try getting the hand more forward. They quietly fight for a bit until Jonathan wins and his hand seems to control Evan's. A smirk is on the winner's face as a shameful, but cute blush goes across Vanoss's face.

Hand in hand, Evan leads Jonathan to the truck of the bearded man. Delirious turns and notices that Luke is gone. Before he could advice Evan the truck door was already open for him. "What about Luke?"

"He let me use his truck for our date," Evan smiles and god damn does it nearly send Delirious back through those hospital doors. He smiles back at him as he hops into the truck with the owl. They drive off from the hospital, a place that Jonathan hopefully will not be going back to in a while.

"Where are we going?" The clown questions as he removes his face from the open window. His wacky brown hair makes Evan chuckle before answering him, "You'll have to wait and see."

"Oh come on! I hate surprises!" Jonathan whines, but Evan couldn't believe that; he plays millions of horror games, how could he hate surprises?

"No, you're just impatient," replies the owl as he turns up the radio. They grow quiet again; enjoying the music and nice breeze from the open windows.

The car stops randomly and Evan gets out. Jonathan lifts his head up and realizes they're at a store, but not just any store. Before he can ask, Vanoss is out of the truck and inside of the music store. Why in the hell would he be at one of these? Is this apart of the date? Jonathan wonders and finally hops out of the truck.

The door makes a jingle as he pushes through. He spots Evan, of course, in the string section. "What are you doing?" Jonathan steps up beside him. Evan taps his chin, "I'm buying a guitar, what's it look like?" He smirks as he points at a tan colored acoustic with purple in the center.

Evan places the instrument in the back of the truck right behind the front seats. Jonathan watches him and notices a picnic basket beside the guitar. A burst of warmth flows into his chest. Is Evan really this sweet? Evan Fong, like VanossGaming? Jonathan smiles and buckles up as Evan pulls out of the parking lot.

Towns and houses gradually disappear during the ride. The black truck finally pulls into another parking lot. Evan grabs the guitar and the basket. "Need any help?" Delirious offers, but Vanoss turns it down and gestures for him to follow with the guitar.

They make their way up a slight hill with a tall oak tree at the top. Jonathan's face hurts from smiling so much at this cliché date. Evan places out a blanket and the basket. The oak tree is big enough for both of them to lean on it. They had a terrific view of the rest of the park. The food looks delicious! Evan Fong definitely has the touch.

As they both eat Jonathan starts a conversation on the guitar, "What's that for?" Evan turns the the black cased instrument. He sets down his sub, "Well, when you touch the strings right it makes a pretty noise-"

"I know what it does douche bag, but why is it here?"

"Wanna figure that out now?" Evan questions with a smug look. Jonathan's face goes red, "Sure!"

"Here," Vanoss motions for Delirious to move closer to him. Jonathan leans on the tree. This position gives Evan an idea. He grabs the guitar and stands up. "Spread your legs," Vanoss demands. The blue eyes widen, but listen. He laughs as he adjusts his legs. "Not like that you pervert," Evan jokes and then sits in between his date's legs. He's so warm and cuddly, but Evan wants to teach him the basics of guitar for their first date. "Here, lemme-" Vanoss murmurs as he grabs Delirious's hands one at a time. He pulls them around his hips and to the guitar. They both blush as Evan moves his fingers with Jonathan's. He smiles as the clown slowly gets used to it, and he pushes him when he messes up. Soon the sun seems to hide. Evan puts the guitar away for now and he leans back. Jonathan nervously gulps, but he wraps his arms around Evan and squeezes him close. They sit and watch the sun gradually disappear. The last remaining rays shine on the blue and brown eyes. Smiles fresh on their lips. Evan tilts his head up and stares at Jonathan. The raccoon moves his head down and their lips connect. Both of their eyes slowly close and they cherish the warm kiss.

***

Questions

Everyone considers "losing your virginity" in different ways. Some people think same sex people can't, but really your virginity is just a thought. It's not something physical. In Jonathan's own mind he's already lost his virginity. Once your skin touches another human's in a sexual way; that's it.

That one time at the park with Weston when Jonathan jacked him off and they kissed and kissed as their hands traveled onto each other's bodies.

Evan sits up and grabs an object from the picnic basket. A little green lantern. He clicks it on and the small light illuminates on both their faces. Jonathan smiles and they sit together once again. "Let's play truths," Delirious offers. Evan can't help, but chuckle, "What are we 12 year old girls?" Jonathan playfully smacks him on the back and scoffs, "No! We could learn more about each other! How about... We call it "questions", aight?"

"Alright," Vanoss finally agrees and moves himself in front of the older man. They stare each other down. "Who first?" Jonathan questions. Evan smirks, "You came up with the idea. Ask me first." Delirious bites his lips as he thinks of a question for the man sitting in front of him. What does the raccoon want to learn about the owl? Let's start small, "What's your favorite color?" A shy smile goes across the tan lips as he thinks. "Yellow, but a really light yellow not that bright yellow, almost faded yellow," Evan explains with the same half smile. Jonathan laughs at his explanation of yellow.

"At what age did you figure out you were bi?"

"13, 14. Who all are you out to?" Jonathan's question seems to take a slight turn. Evan frowns a little and sighs, "You and Luke..."

"Seriously? So..."

"You're the first one to know..."

"Your parents?"

"It's my turn to ask a question Delirious!"

"Okay! Okay!" Delirious raises his hands like Evan is going to arrest him or shoot him. The owl sighs, "Have you listened to any of my music?"

"Holy shit, yes! Are you kidding? My best friend is making music! Of course I'd listen to it. Sorry if I never like posted about it like the other guys did, but goddamn your guitar solo. You're amazing!" Evan watches Delirious's eyes light up as he speaks about his own music. It blows the owl away. He had no idea.

"How'd you feel about our first kiss?"

Evan's eyes widen at this question, "Surprised. I loved it. It was like a dream come true. It was like a love story; you risked your damn life for me." Jonathan genuinely smiles and grabs Evan's hand. The brown eyes crawl up to the blue ones, "Are you a virgin?"

"No," he seems to purr. "Have you ever had sex with a man?"

"No..." Evan's voice disappears as Jonathan inches closer to him. His hand grabs onto Delirious's thigh as their lips connect. Jonathan grabs Evan's by the thighs and lifts him on over his own legs. His back falls against the tree and his hands travel up the white shirt of Evan's. Jonathan pulls the head hole of the Metallica shirt and starts kissing his neck. Evan groans as Jonathan's kisses slowly turn into nibbles. He grabs his wrist and pauses his kisses. The innocent brown eyes connect with the loving blue ones, "Are you sure you want to do this?" Evan questions as he traces Delirious's face. The blue eyes slowly blink and as the man nods. Pallid hands unbutton the dark skinny jeans of the owl. As Jonathan's hand slips under his lover's jeans, Evan's lips meet his warm pair and the move down to his neck. With each thrust of his hand, the harder Evan bites onto Delirious's neck. His teeth send shrills through his body. He couldn't believe he's pleasing the hottest and sweetest man on Earth. Jonathan smiles at the wonderful noise of Evan's heavy breathing. Soon, he's close to his climax. "Faster, faster!" Evan orders in a gruttal whisper. He obeys; Jonathan's ears nearly explode to the sonorous noise of the younger man's moan. He dark hair swings back with him as he throws his head back. His white teeth shines as he smiles in satisfaction. The little lantern shines in the blue eyes as he smirks at his pleased date.

After using a few napkins, Evan ends up between Jonathan's legs again, but this time with the guitar. He strums on it and quietly hums along with it. The blue eyes search the night sky for stars as he listens to Evan's playing. "Can you sing?" Delirious randomly questions. His eyes are removed from the sky and Evan stops playing. He flips himself around and gives Delirious a daring glare, "Why?"

"Because, I've always wanted to hear you sing," Jonathan admits with a goofy smile, tainted with a blush. "I mean... I could try," Evan offers. He'd do anything for Delirious. "Any song request?" Jonathan's eyes fill with wonder as he digs through his favorite songs in his head. He smiles as he answers, "Wonderwall?"

"Really? Alright..." Evan starts playing his guitar. If the song had a bunch of crickets in the background it would have been spot on. "Today is gonna be the day that they're gonna throw it back to you. By now you should've somehow..." as Evan continues singing Jonathan seems to fall into his dark chocolate eyes. Maybe Evan's going to be the one to save me... Delirious smiles pierced ear to pierced ear. "I don't believe that anybody feels the way I do, about you now-" Evan stops playing and looks around. "What?" Jonathan worries. "Shh, did you hear that?"

"What?"

"Somebody's here with us..."

"Evan stop fucking around-"

"Jonathan? Evan?" The oh-so terrible familiar voice questions in the dark. Evan stands up defensively and storms toward the dark figure. Jonathan gets up quickly after him, he takes the lantern with him. He lifts it up to the mysterious figure's face. His septum piercing shimmers and his bleach blond hair sticks out like a sore thumb. "Weston? What the fuck are you doing here?" Vanoss's voice seems to have changed into a damn demon. Before Weston could answer Evan growls in again, "You better stay the fuck away from Jonathan!" He pokes at the intruder's chest. Weston falls back a few steps, "Woah, calm down there, I just wanted to-"

"He forgot you! Remember?! Why bother him again?!" Evan snaps. Even though both of them knew, Jonathan and Evan, that he had remembered Weston earlier today. Jonathan tries stepping in between them when Weston takes a big step toward Evan. Daring brown eyes meet each other. Jonathan's hands rest on each man's chest, "Stop it, both of you!" They seem to get closer, pushing Jonathan away from them. "He chose me. Get the fuck out of here."

"But I was here first."

"Then why'd you dump him all those years ago?"

"Ya know what? Fuck you Evan Fong!' Weston growls. Who'd win? An owl or a bull? The poor raccoon steps back as Weston finally gets the balls to punch Evan in the chest. He staggers backward. When he looks up a warm heat goes through Delirious's body. His eyes seem dangerous and Jonathan loves that look on him, but didn't want either of them getting hurt. "Guys please don't-!" Evan runs and tackles Weston down by his waist. They tumble down the hill. Jonathan runs after them, cursing at them for fighting.

He's never had two men fight over him before.

This has to be a dream.

Part of Jonathan hopes it is a dream, but the other half kinda doesn't. It's hot watching Evan throw punches at Delirious's ex...

***

Fight

Evan has never fought anyone physically once in his life. In hockey he might have gotten a little aggressive, but that's it. If it wasn't for hockey he would be jello right now.

Weston swings again and punches Evan right in the nose. Something cracks and blood starts dripping. He ignores this and punches Weston in the chest multiple times until he falls over again. "Stop fucking fighting!" Delirious shouts again, but both men ignore him and continue pushing and shoving. Vanoss pushes Weston hard on the shoulders. So hard he falls backwards down the slight hill. Jonathan groans and follows the bleeding Evan down the hill. Weston thankfully stands up and swings at the closest target. He punches Delirious right in the jaw. Triggering his concussion. The man falls to his knees as his works goes dark. Evan freaks out and grabs Weston by the collar. Evan rounds his arm up and punches Weston so hard that his piercing actually leaves a gash in Vanoss's knuckles and the man goes unconscious with a black eye. Evan groans and falls beside Delirious, "Oh no, come on. Get up." Jonathan moans in pain, but uses all of his strength to lift himself up. He knows there's no way in hell Vanoss could carry him to the truck.

"Here, you stay in here and I'll go grab our stuff," Evan explains, but before rushing off Jonathan grabs his hand. The brown eyes whip around, "What's wrong?"

"Your nose... Why'd you do it?"

"What?"

"Fight him," a half awake Delirious answers. Vanoss sadly smiles and places Jonathan's hand on his sore cheek. He sighs, "Because, no one can mess with my Delirious." Evan walks away, leaving a smiling Delirious.

When Evan starts up the hill he notices that Weston must have left. A dark feeling hits him. Like a weight is put on his shoulders. Why did he fight with him? There's no reason to...

A knock on the window scares Delirious. He turns and meets Weston. He frowns and rolls down the window. "Are you alright?" He immediately asks. Delirious nods, "Yeah, my head hurts a little bit. Are you alright?"

"Yeah, my nose is broken, I think. I'm so sorry for approaching you guys. You were obviously on a date."

"It's okay. You know, I remember who you are, and I'm sorry."

"What are you sorry for? I'm the one who broke up with you. For a stupid career I didn't even achieve..."

"I thought you did," Delirious places his arm on the frame of the window. Weston frowns and bites his lip, "I- Uh, didn't..." Jonathan shifts in his seat. He pulls his shirt over his hips and below his rear-end. "What do you mean you didn't? You told me you ran a clothing line for plus size men... For me," Jonathan explains with a little confusion in his voice. Weston sobs, "I work at the fucking drive thru at McDonald's... I gave up that dream when

I realized I gave up something that meant more to me. I also had terrible ideas."

"Why'd you lie to me then?" Jonathan's hand tightens on the window frame. "Because... I don't know. I wanted to seem cool to you."

"Liars aren't cool."

"Jonathan I'm sorry I lied."

"You broke up with me for something you didn't even do. Then you quit the thing you wanna do because you realized I was more important!?" Jonathan's voice cracks, "You made me feel terrible after you left. I felt disgusting. Fat. Ugly."

"Jonathan..."

"Weston, please don't come near me again. I don't want to see you."

"Fine you fat ass!" Weston shouts and it echoes throughout the park. The sound of a fragile heart breaks too. Tears stream out of the ocean eyes. Anger boils in his blood. "YOU NEVER LOVED ME YOU BIG. FAT. LIAR!" Delirious yells and jumps out of the truck. His hands wrap around Weston's neck. Jonathan gets close to him after pinning him on the ground. His mouth barely moves with his threatening words, "You used the thing you know I'm most sensitive about against me. I may be fat, but at least I'm not an asshole."

Evan sprints down the hill with the date stuff. He rushes over to Delirious pinning Weston down. Suddenly Evan is feeling what Jonathan was feeling a little while ago; hot. The lustful feeling disappears when Evan notices that Jonathan's hands are wrapped around Weston's neck. He drops the stuff and runs over. He pushes Delirious off. They tumble over. Evan places his hands on Jonathan's chest. Jonathan heavily sighs and wraps his arms around him.

Weston coughs and stands up. He spits and storms away from the couple. Hopefully never to be seen again.

In the truck ride home Evan questions Delirious about the fight, "Why'd you two go at it?"

"He, uh," he sighs and runs his fingers through his wacky brown hair. Evan frowns at him, "You don't have to tell me."

"No, we need to start being true each other," Jonathan demands and clears his throat, "He called me a fat ass and I flipped, because he's always called me things that meant the opposite."

"He's an asshole," Evan chuckles, "plus he's wrong. You're awesome, handsome. Your size is the best. I love it. I love you for you. You're an amazing cuddler by the way." Jonathan smiles and grabs Evan's hand in the center console, "Thanks. Your lips are amazing. Their life soft cookies as soon as they get out of the oven." Laughter fills the truck as it speeds away from the park.

"WHERE WERE YOU? I WAS WORRIED SICK ABOUT Y'ALL!" CaRtOoNz stands in the center of the doorway to Jonathan's house. His hands on his hips and his angry face placed. As the boys walk in he stops both of them. "Evan, what the hell happened to your nose? Delirious your fucking cheek is bruised!" He pushes them into the house and slams the door shut.

They sit on to the couch and Luke's lecture begins, "What the hell happened?" Like innocent children, Evan and Jonathan turn and look at each other before answering Luke, "Weston found us."

"You're fucking kiddin' me!"

"I fought with him first," Evan admits.

"First?!" Luke's voice cracks as he screeches.

"I fought him second, but he'll never show up here again!" Delirious tries defending himself and Vanoss.

"Y'all are fucking grounded," Luke states seriously, but then he bursts out laughing, "I'm fucking glad y'all took care of him. You guys are a power couple!" They chuckle and intertwine their fingers.

Upstairs in Jonathan's bedroom he finds Evan sprawled out on his bed. "Uh, what are you doin'?"

"Let's continue what we started. Watching you choke out Weston really changed me," Evan purrs, but can't help chuckle at the last part. Jonathan smiles and crawls into bed with him. "All this fighting and fixing after the fighting is really tiring," Jonathan admits, but kisses Evan anyway. He lightly kisses the white bandage over his darkened nose. Evan pulls him in for a deep kiss, some tongue action goes on as well. Suddenly their hands start moving, without their minds attached. Jonathan pulls away quickly and glances at Evan. It's only the first date and they were about to get dirty, plus no one has ever seen him completely naked before. Jonathan swims in deep chocolate eyes. He searches for a hint that Evan is the one. That he'll love Jonathan's body for what it is.

Jonathan has no idea how much Evan truly loves him.

His body is like a beautiful garden to Evan, waiting to be explored and examined for all its extravagant flowers.

***

Pleasing

He's never gotten naked in front of anyone. He could barely look himself in the mirror when he'd shower. He'd stare at himself until the water would run warm enough. He'd trace his hands all over his stomach, wishing each touch would make it smaller, or make himself look hotter. He wishes his chest was smaller as well. That he didn't have a double chin. His arms weren't so wide and his thighs so fat. Evan Fong is going to see him naked for the first time; as a grown man. If he'd let him.

The bruises on Evan's neck were visible, because his t-shirt hole was stretched out by Delirious earlier at the park. Jonathan's hair is still a mess, but so were his feelings about these next events. Seeing Evan sit there so innocently with a stretched out t-shirt and a messed up hairdo made something in Delirious lose everything. "Are you okay?" Vanoss questions with concern. Jonathan slowly nods, but Evan can tell he's lying. "You're lying, what's wrong?" He crawls over to Delirious and grabs his hand, "You can tell me anything..."

"I know. I just- I'm overthinking everything," Delirious explains with a sigh. "What are you thinking about?" This question makes Delirious angry at himself. It's Evan, he's the best thing to happen to him. Showing him his body shouldn't hurt. Tell him the truth.

"I'm afraid to get naked in front of you," he explains in a rush and waits for Evan to reply. Instead of words he gets a long kiss. Once they pull away Evan smiles, "Sex is about pleasing, not looks. To me anyway." Jonathan smiles, realizing that the owl is genuinely speaking. "We can go slow, alright?"

"Yeah," Delirious nods and moves his hand to Evan's jaw. He places a soft kiss, making both of them close their eyes. They stop and open their eyes slowly. The brown eyes look up at the blue ones. Evan falls backwards onto the bed and lays with his legs spread. Jonathan moves over to him on his knees. He grabs Evan's thighs as he kisses him once more. His slightly afraid of putting his weight onto his partner. He tries to ignore this thought as Evan's soft lips move down his neck. Black skinny jeans are unbuttoned along with a blue button up shirt; only a few buttons on the shirt. Evan's kisses continue down Delirious's neck down to his collar bone. Evan then moves back up his face to his ear. His teeth make a quiet clinking noise as they hit Jonathan's piercing. The pale hands run through the raven hair. Evan stops bitting on Delirious's ear to whisper, "I want you to fuck me." His breathe is warm on his ear. His soft, but demanding voice sends chills down the clown's back.

Jonathan's lips stay connected as he shimmies Evan out of his jeans. His lips make the owl's feathers fluff. On his neck Jonathan's kisses make warm sparks fly through Evan's body. A burning sensation starts below both of their waist. Suddenly Vanoss rips the rest of the buttons on Delirious's baby blue, revealing his beautiful chest and stomach. Evan's fingers trace over each stretch mark like they're a pattern in a painting. Jonathan's red face makes Evan pull him down and smash their faces together. Their nose squish together as they violently make out. As their tongues dance, Evan's hands travel down to Delirious's shorts. He slips them off along with his boxers. "Evan!" He gasps an tries covering himself, but Vanoss stops him. "You're beautiful. Now shut up and fuck me," he demands as a huge smirk crawls across both of their faces. Evan stares at Jonathan's boner as he pulls off his boxers to reveal his own. Their eyes meet and the next few moves happen super fast. Jonathan grabs Evan's legs and lifts them high on his hips. Their members touch briefly as they shift in the bed. Evan's hands go up above his head. He clenches onto the pillow as Jonathan questions, "Are you ready?" The brown eyes swim in the ocean blue ones as he nods. This is his first time with a man. Jonathan knew this. He slowly enters into Evan. Evan gasps in pain at first. "Is this alright?"

"Go deeper."

Jonathan obeys and slowly moves his hips forward. Evan then quickly squeezes his legs around Delirious's hips. He gasps with this quick action. "Right there," he basically whispers. Delirious's gut flutters at his tone of voice. His hips move back and forth smoothly. He watches Evan clench onto the pillows beneath his head. His breathing becomes heavier as Delirious grinds his hips. Hearing Vanoss breathe heavily and move his head back and forth made Delirious's senses run wild. Evan's legs squeeze again and his breathing gets faster. "Faster, faster!" He shouts and balls the pillow cases in his hands. Their heavy breathing matches in beat. Like a marching band in tempo. Each thrust with each heavy gasp. Jonathan watches Evan's mouth open the slightest and his eyes squeeze shut. His legs squash Jonathan's hips as he orgasms and cums over Jonathan's stomach. He throws his head back, sweat flipping off his hair. The smallest moan leaves his soft lips followed by the slightest, "Jonathan." This sets off the older man. His brown hair drips with sweat as he climaxes inside Evan. Brown eyes open in time to see the blue eyes fly backwards as he moans; almost mumbles. He removes himself from Evan, but stays on his knees. They meet in the middle and kiss for the longest time. Their lips connect like puzzle pieces.

Vanoss flinches as he falls back on the pillow. "Oh no," Delirious chuckles as he lays beside him. "I think that's gonna hurt, but you'll get used to it," he teases again. Vanoss scoffs, "You think you're so dominant, but who was shouting demands?" They both chuckle. "You just fucked me out of my mind, Jonathan..." he states and places a thumb on the bottom of Delirious's lip. They stare at each other and play with each other's lips or hair until one of them eventually falls asleep. Delirious moves himself closer to Vanoss. He wraps his arms around him and hugs him close. Theblue eyes examine the sleeping man. He removes one hand from his chest and runs his fingers through his hair one last time, "What do you see in me Evan Fong?" Delirious doesn't understand how much the little owl truly loves him. How much he appreciates his body. How much he adores his laugh and personality. Evan loves him.*** Guess who's not dead?

Sorry.

Two Months

After Jonathan's secret was released he felt very uncomfortable around his father. He never really said anything about it after the punishment. Maybe his father really didn't care; that's what he hoped. The grown 31-year-old man doesn't even talk to his dad. He knows he's still alive, because he keeps in touch with his mother and two other siblings. Jonathan doesn't know if he'll ever see his dad again; now that he has a boyfriend, again.

Evan tries to keep in touch with his parents as much as he can. He hasn't told anyone of them yet about his sexuality or Jonathan. Maybe Evan should reach out to his uncles first, ask his mother's brother how he came out.

Remember the fact that Jonathan would never see his father again? Keep that in mind...

"Are we going to do anything special for Labor Day?" Luke questions as he pours himself a glass of orange juice from Delirious's fridge. The man glares at him for taking his drink, but then he turns to Evan with a goofy look on his face, "Any idea?"

"Nope, I've got nothing." They all sigh in defeat. "I mean, I have a pool. We can hang there? Just us," Luke offers. "We can get alcohol, cards, different games, a volleyball. Ya know? Food."

"Foooooooooood," Delirious quotes himself. They chuckle at their plan and agree to it. CaRtOoNz rushes out of the kitchen to grab a notebook to make a list of things they'll need to get. Once he's gone the couple turns to each other and give each other a goofy smile. Their hands, by instinct, connect and intertwine. Evan smiles and then sighs, "So, when are we going to tell Luke that we fucked for the first time two months ago?" The blue eyes widen and the free pale hand punches Evan in the arm. "No! He'll kill me!"

"Why?" Evan questions with a cheeky smile. Jonathan thinks back to that moment. The look on Evan's face, his quiet moans. At the time he thought he were dreaming. Evan's the most fit man on the fucking planet, and then Jonathan looks like a "before" picture from those Weight Watchers' commercials. He sighs, but a hand squeeze makes him look up into those wonderful brown eyes. "We don't have to tell him anything. We don't even have to tell the boys." Honestly, both of them forgot about YouTube for a little bit. It'd be neat if they both would play together more often and update. They should come back strong. A few game ideas pop into the head of the clown.

"I haven't talked to any of the guys in a while..." Jonathan shamefully admits and rubs his thumb on Evan's fingers. Suddenly the clown's phone rings. Vanoss frowns as Jonathan's hand disconnects from his. Jonathan grabs his black framed glasses and slips them on to read the caller ID. "Hmm," he mumbles and steps out of the kitchen to talk.

Vanoss sits there and wonders who is on the phone with him, and why he had to move away. He sighs and stares at the orange juice sitting on the table.

In the living room Jonathan greets his sister, "Jenny?"

"Jon?! You're alive!"

"Yeah, no shit. Why'd you call?"

"To see if you were okay, and... well, Mom's invited us over for Labor day. Dad's gonna-"

"Dad," the name sounds like poison on Jonathan's tongue. Jenny rolls her blue eyes and sighs into the phone, "Johnny please. Dad won't care-"

"I have a boyfriend though. I'd love to take him over to meet Mom, and you and Sam!"

"What?! You have a boy and you didn't tell me?!" Her voice seems to get louder as she speaks. Jonathan pulls the phone away from his ear as she rants. He smiles and brings the phone back, "I'm sorry. You remember that Vanoss guy I was talking to you about like 4 years ago at Christmas?"

"Yeah! Oh my god! It's him?! No way!" Laughter mixes between both of them until the line grows silent again. "So, are you coming down?"

"I don't know..."

"Jon, please. I think you should," Jenny begs. What Delirious didn't know was the fact that his Dad only had a month or so to live. His body is slowly shutting down, because of alcohol and smoking. Jenny frowns and hopes to God Jon will come over. He needs to see him one last time.

"Dad's changed," she explains, and she wasn't really wrong. Delirious sighs, "I guess. I'll have to cancel plans with Evan and Luke then."

"Fuck Luke," she spats in a joking tone. They laugh again and then Jonathan hangs up.

He strolls back into the kitchen to a smiling CaRtOoNz and Vanoss. He notices the long list and solemnly smiles, "Well, we have to cancel our plans for this weekend?" Luke looks like he just watched a cat get his by a truck and Vanoss looks like he was just handed a test he had no idea about.

"What?! Why!?" Luke whines and slams his hand on the table. "We're going over to my parents for Labor day." Evan's jaw drops, which then slowly turns into a smile. Luke's face pictures a lot of worry, about Jonathan going back. He hasn't talked to his dad in thirteen years, and he really isn't looking forward to it.

Throughout the evening the two pack their bags as Luke makes plans with other friends. Evan just repacks his whole suitcase, since he hasn't really brought his stuff down from his home yet. Jonathan worries about his boyfriend. Anxiety rises in his throat like a deadly disease. Maybe he should hide the fact Evan is his boyfriend, but that's a terrible idea. Fuck it. A sudden punch of rebellion hits the 31-year-old. Hell, maybe they'd even fuck in his old bedroom- No terrible idea Delirious. Or is it? Jonathan looks up at Evan and smiles. He returns the cute smile as they finish up packing. They crawl into bed together and prepare themselves for the short trip tomorrow.

Just before falling asleep Evan mumbles, "I love you." And flips away from Jonathan, pushing himself into his arms. Those words with his voice toward Jonathan made him replay the saying in his head over and over again. He wonders why he does as he wraps his arms around Evan's hips. He nuzzles his nose into the back of his head, "I love you too."

***

Updates are sorta slow. Trying to get on a schedule to fit around marching band and school. I love y'all.

- HoodiniClown

Meeting

"Honey, you can love whoever you want, okay?"

"Yes, I know Mom. It's not you I'm worried about," as the 20-year-old Jonathan speaks he turns to his father sitting on the couch. His eyes glued onto the TV. Mrs. Dennis sighs at her son. She wraps her arms around him. As she speaks her voice vibrates on Jonathan's shoulder, "He'll come around soon baby."

Did he really?

"Are you ready?" Jonathan questions as Evan sits on the couch with his luggage beside him. He looks up from his phone and nods. He seems very quiet.

In the car, Delirious tries figuring out why. "Are you alright?" At a traffic light the truck of Luke's pulls to a stop. Evan turns over to Jonathan, his hands tight on the steering wheel. "I'm just nervous," he shrugs and continues driving. His eyes being removed from Delirious's. The blue eyes examine the owl, looking for some kind of sign as to why he is nervous. The silence nearly kills the two in the vehicle. Evan sighs and turns on the stereo, "Can you plug my phone in please?" Jonathan hums a yes and plugs the red cased phone into the truck. Jonathan just hits "shuffle" on Vanoss's phone. The first song starts off slow and then Delirious realizes this is the song he did a remix to recently. "Is this-"

"Cry by Alison Wonderland," Evan answers for him. He turns with a smirk across his face. Delirious chuckles, "I like it." The two continue jamming out in the car, no care in the world.

"In 25 feet turn left," the GPS shouts at the driver, Evan. He takes a deep breath as he turns onto Jonathan's childhood road. While they go slow down the road, a hand crawls over Evan's. Their fingers hug each other. Blue eyes connect with brown. The pale hand squeezes around the tan fingers. Jonathan searches for the familiar gray house; nostalgia kicks in. Good memories crash with bad ones. A sigh is released from the older man. Vanoss squeezes back and shoots him a cheeky smile. Jonathan smiles back. Their gaze stops when he points at a driveway entrance. Lavender bushes sit at each edge. Three cars sit in the driveway already. A small blue pickup truck closest to the house; a black mini-van sits beside the truck; behind the truck sits a red punch bug, so Evan pulls in beside the bug. After taking the key out, Evan sighs and plops back in his seat. "Are you ready to meet my family?" Evan nods as Jonathan places a kiss on his lips. They pull away and smile at each other once again. Evan sighs and opens the truck door.   Before Evan can open the back of the truck for his luggage, Jonathan stops him. A confused look goes across Vanoss's face. "Let's greet them first. I'm just gonna come out and say you're my boyfriend," Delirious explains. Evan's stomach suddenly drops and his heart rate goes up, "Really?" Jonathan grabs his forearm and rubs it, "Do you not want me to?" Evan shakes his head, "No, we need to get this over with. We shouldn't have to hide this," Evan gestures to their intertwined hands. Jon's heart warms, along with his cheeks. He grabs the back of Evan's head and pushes his lips onto his into a hard kiss.

The couple finally make their way up to the front door that Jonathan used to walk through everyday. A sigh escapes the lips of the older man as his knuckles tap on the door. Evan squeezes his hand for reassurance. The door slowly opens, a short woman with short brown locks with little streaks here and there; her blue eyes are ten times lighter than her youngest son's. They seem to tear up as she stares at her son and his wonderful boyfriend. "Johnny?" Her voice cracks with his name. She breaks down as she throws her arms around her Jonathan. Evan's heart shatters as he watches the two reunite. As they pull away someone else sneaks out the front door. His pepper hair seems to match his dark face expression, "Who is this?" He gestures toward Evan. Mrs. Dennis hugs Evan and Jonathan smirks at his boyfriend. "This is my boyfriend, Evan," he states loud and clear. Evan's face flusters. Jonathan risked his father's love for his own. Evan was sure as hell gonna marry this man. His father shakes his head at his son and walks back into the house. Mrs. Dennis pulls away and sadly smiles, "Don't worry about him, sweetie. He'll eventually get over it. Come on in!" The couple follows the woman into the house. Evan is greeted by a girl with long brown hair and the same blue eyes. She smiles and immediately wraps her arms around Evan without saying anything. They stay there for a second and then she whispers, "Thanks for saving my brother."

Later on Evan sits on the couch and thinks to himself as Jonathan helps his family in the kitchen with dinner. He sighs and moves his red solo cup of alcohol; he listens to the sound it makes as it swishes around the plastic cup. All of a sudden Jonathan's father comes inside from the back porch. Evan immediately sits up and tries to flash him a smile, but the man seems to have a deadpan look on his face. The man sits into a chair that seems to have a marking in it from him sitting in it and doing nothing over the 31 years of his son's life. A gruttal noise makes the owl jump. The sound of Mr. Dennis clearing his throat frightens the young adult. "Evan, is it?"

"Yeah," Evan pretty much squeaks. Mr. Dennis shifts in his chair, turning himself toward Evan. "So, you're the one with my son?"

"Yes, I am."

"I'm sorry." This comment confuses Evan. Isn't that something for Jonathan to hear?

"I think you should talk to Jonathan."

"Can I talk to you Evan?"

"Uh, sure." Both of them make their way out onto the front porch. They surprisingly share the same swing on the porch. They're quiet for a little while, until Evan decides to speak up, "So, what'd you want to talk to me about?" He sighs and a slight smile comes across his face, "I want to get to know the man that changed my son's life."

Inside Jonathan and Jenny help out their mother with dinner. As Jonathan cuts up the cheese for pasta salad he notices a Dennis missing. "Where's Sam? I saw his car outside, but I don't see him, or Megan." Jonathan doesn't see it, but Jenny gives her mother a smile. "I think they're upstairs still unpacking their stuff for this weekend," Jenny only half lies. They were really upstairs getting a surprise ready for Jonathan. He wouldn't see it until dinner though. The women laugh and Jonathan gets a little flustered, because he's left out.

"I was so stupid back then. I hated everything, everyone, for no good reason. I missed half of my son's life, just because of who he loved," tears were slipping out of the blue eyes of Mr. Dennis as he pours out his sorrows. "Mr. Dennis, it's okay-"

"Call me Dad, Evan. Please." Evan's heart nearly explodes and his ears start ringing at the thought of him and Jon ever getting married, or the thought of one of them proposing. Evan did love Jonathan, he's 100% sure.

Jonathan could be a psychopath killer and Evan would still love him to death. The words seem to flow out of his mouth, "Can I have your blessing to marry your wonderful son?"

*** Eyo! I apologise for the lack of updates.

I'mma come clean now; this book and Want You are the last H2OVanoss books I'm going to write for a very long time, probably forever. I'm moving on to legitimate books. I'm definitely still in the fandom, but I won't be writing about them anymore.

I love all of you.

I thank you for coming the far with me. <3

The Question

Jonathan has always dreamt of how a man would propose to him as a child, especially when he met Weston. What would Weston do? How would he propose? Would Jonathan propose?

What if Jonathan met a girl he liked?

A hormonal Jonathan would imagine Weston taking him on a romantic dinner and then to an arcade to spend the rest of the night, and then at home, he'd get down on one knee right outside his doorstep and would pop the question.

Obviously, that will never happen.

Evan's got different plans.

It is now October of the year 2019, Jonathan and Evan have been together for a little over a year now. Their families have met and love one another. Everything seemed to be going fine, except for the fact the owl is going a little insane. Even after the fact he finally came out to his family. His father accepted him, merely because he only cared for Evan and was glad he was doing okay as an adult and it really doesn't matter who he loves coming home to after a day of work.

Jonathan is currently resting in bed with a sinus infection, while Evan taps his foot in the dining room searching on his laptop. He waits for a reply from his extended family members. He really needed this one's help. While he waits he scrolls through a store on another tab; a jeweler to be exact. It has to be perfect, Vanoss thinks to himself. He chooses different categories; statement rings, bands, men. He sighs and shakes to the thought of his own hands sliding the ring onto Jonathan's finger. A small smile goes across his face as he plays different scenarios in his head. As he's searching his computer dings. His heart jumps as he switches to the other tab and notices the name Eric Crane flashing. Evan clicks on it and realizes his uncle is free to talk. He clicks on the little camera button and waits. He cracks his knuckles and turns down the volume, just in case Delirious wakes up.

An oh-so-familiar face appears on the computer screen. He has the matching brown eyes of his older sister and a genuine smile on his face. His cheekbones are high and his dark hair is gelled up nice.

"Hello, Evan, what's the matter?" His voice sent shrills of excitement through his body. He felt like a 12-year-old again. During the video call, Evan explains Jonathan's story to him. His uncle smiles, frowns and gives plenty of feedback. "That's straight out of a freaking Hallmark movie. That's amazing Evan, I'm so glad you found someone. Your mother actually told me about you recently. I wish I had the balls you did to come out to your parents. I was pushed out by your mother," he chuckles and rubs his neck. He sighs, "So, what's going on with you two now? Where's he at?"

"Well, he's up in bed resting, he's got a terrible sinus infection, so I figured it was a good time to look for a ring..."

Evan doesn't need to look up to see his uncle covering his mouth and flapping his hand around. After his little exciting fit, Eric finally speaks, "So how are you going to do it?"

Upstairs Jonathan groans as he coughs himself awake. "Fuck," he mumbles; phlegm living in his throat. His ear still hurt and his nose was still stuffed. The heating pad didn't seem to be working very well. Jonathan didn't see Evan around and suddenly grew worried, like a baby he wanted to cry for him. Instead, he threw the blanket off of him and turned on the TV. He feels like shit, he didn't want to do anything, but cuddle with Evan and watch reruns of The Golden Girls. Evan has other plans that are the total opposite of what Jonathan wants to do, but neither of them has any idea.

"Thank you so much, Eric, I miss talking to you! Tell Greg I said hello!" Evan shuts the laptop and rushes upstairs to tell his love that he had to run out quick to grab a few "things". The door creaks open into the small cave of Delirious's. Tissues, blankets, and wrappers lay everywhere in the room. The TV flickers onto the bed, making it change colors with different scenes. Delirious's head peeks out over the blanket. "Hey, are you feeling any better?" Evan sits on the edge of the bed and starts rubbing Jonathan's legs. He sits up a little bit, making room for Evan to climb onto the bed at the bottom. He sighs, "I'm definitely feeling better than before, my throat and ears are still botherin' me." To Evan, his voice still sounds so different, almost like someone poured water over his microphone and stuffed rocks in his throat. "Well, I was thinking about going out tonight for dinner, but it can wait," Evan only half lies; dinner could wait, but could the proposal?

"No, let's go out. I may be a little sick. Going out might actually help me."

"Jonathan are you sure?" The owl questions and continues rubbing his legs. He groans, "Yes, I'm sure. I wouldn't miss a dinner with you for anything." They both smile. Evan climbs up the rest of the way onto the bed and places a kiss on Jonathan's plump lips. They sit in silence as their eyes glue to each other. Evan notices the alarm clock beside Jonathan says 2:43; he needs to go pick up a ring. He sighs, "I still need to make a quick trip. Why don't you rest a little more while I'm gone, is that okay?"

"Yeah, I need to finish this episode of The Golden Girls anyway." Evan turns to the TV screen and chuckles, "This is why I fucking love you," they kiss once more and Vanoss climbs off the bed.

"Evan!" Delirious yells before the owl sneaks out the bedroom door. The brown-eyed man whips around, "Yes?"

"Be careful!"

"Always."

Evan had gotten Jonathan's ring size from his mother after he asked his father for his blessing a few months back.

Evan couldn't help himself, he keeps peeking at the black diamond ring. His nerves were starting to get the best of him; what if he says no? What if the ring doesn't fit? What if I drop it?

Evan shakes his head and drives to the nearest grocery outlet.

Jonathan laughs at another remark of Rose's as he digs through his dresser to find clothes for tonight. He and Evan didn't really go on dinner dates. They consider every moment with each other a date. Jonathan didn't like going out either. That meant dressing up, making sure he didn't look fat in the dress shirt he would be wearing. Making sure he looked as thin as possible. Even with Evan around Jonathan still hates the way he looks...

He runs his fingers through his gelled up brown hair. It's slickness shining in the bathroom light. His piercing blue eyes look at his ears, black studs cleaned, along with the hole for the piercing. The black button-up looks half decent on him. The electric blue bow tie doesn't look too bad either. He smiles at the memory attached to them.

"Jonathan! Get ready for the best birthday of your life!" Evan cheers and jumps on the bed. The smell of breakfast streams through the nostrils of the older man. "I'm only turning thirty-two, calm down."

"But it's your birthday! Jonathan Lee Dennis's birthday! The love of my life! Get up! I've got multiple surprises for you today!"

Jonathan gets himself ready for the day in the bathroom. He notices a blue object with a sticky note attached to it. "First gift! Can't wait to take this off of you tonight! ;)". A smile crawls across his face as he examines the tie. His fingers glide over the silk feeling of it.

He's basically wearing the outfit he did on his first birthday celebrated with Vanoss. He happily sighs and rushes out of the bathroom as soon as he hears the front door slam. The time is currently 4:07.

He spots Evan down the staircase unloading things in the kitchen. Evan turns around and a huge smile goes across his face. The same smile that appears every time he sees Delirious. The brown eyes seem to almost glow toward Delirious. The blue eyes swallow Evan like the ocean sweeping someone in from the shore. After their speechless fit and Jonathan dramatic entrance, they finally meet and quickly kiss. "Are you ready?" Vanoss questions.

"More than ready. I took Dayquil, nothing's stopping me now."

"You're a fucking dork," Evan chuckles as he grabs everything he needs for his proposal. They make their way to the car and Evan's nerves seem to continue jumping up and down. He takes a deep breath before getting into his little red sports car. He speeds off towards their favorite café in North Carolina.

Jonathan realizes where they're at when he sees the party lights hanging outside and the cute blue umbrellas sitting at each table. Evan opens the door for him, surprising the clown. He smiles and takes his strong hand.

They walk into the shop, hand in hand. People stare. Some smile. Some ignore. Jonathan hadn't realized it before, but there's no one sitting outside, which is very unusual. He ignores that weird feeling and follows Evan and the waitress outside.

"Here's your table, I'll be right out to serve you lovely gentleman."

They both sit down and open the menus. "What do you feel like trying tonight?" Evan questions as he flips through the menu. Jonathan smirks at him and looks down, "I might get the pepperoni rolls for an appetizer."

"Oh shit, good thinking."

The waitress comes out and grabs their drink orders, "Are you guys ready to order yet?"

"No, just a few more minutes please," Jonathan answers, "but we would like to try your pepperoni rolls as an appetizer."

"Alrighty," she scribbles in her little notebook and walks off.

Jonathan goes back to flipping through the menu again. He misses the glance between Evan and the waitress as she disappears back into the building. "I think I might try the steak," Evan announces. Jonathan looks up in surprise, "I've never seen you eat steak."

"I mean, I don't eat it a lot. It's a special occasion..." Evan sorta mumbles the last part. "What was that?" Delirious questions, but Evan, of course, ignores him and continues skimming the menu. The clown sighs and searches his menu as well.

The waitress brings water for them to start and their appetizer. "Are two ready to order as well?" The waitress smiles, her green eyes shimmering with excitement. "Yes, we are," Evan replies with a wink at the waitress.

Jonathan taps his fingers on the table, "So, any new song ideas or anything?"

"Well, I haven't had time to work on the music itself, but I have been scribbling down lyrics."

"Oh, so that's what that book is on your bedside! I had no idea you wrote lyrics."

"Yeah. I haven't touched my guitar in a while."

A pause grows between the couple.

"What if you moved in with me? I mean you basically are, but... we've been dating for a year and a half almost." The heart of the younger man seems to burn; in a good way. He needs to propose soon. Lisa, the waitress, is in charge of the song Evan picked out for his proposal. As if Lisa could read his mind, the song playing in the cafe suddenly changed and grew louder. The Good Side by Troye Sivan, the song that was playing when Jonathan chased the train and kissed Evan. It's when they both confessed their love.

Jonathan realizes the music gets louder, he also notices the artist and the song. He looks around for the source but is stopped when his hand is grabbed. He turns to Evan, their eyes locking. "Jonathan Dennis. The man of my dreams, sometimes the man of my nightmare..." Delirious stares at Evan with a furrowed brow. He doesn't say anything and lets Evan continue, "You've changed my life, you beautiful man. I want you to change the rest of my life as well..." Vanoss lets go of his hand and stands up beside the table. He reaches in the back of his pocket; this it clicks for Jonathan. His right hand comes up to his lips, covering his open mouth. Evan pulls out the black box and gets down onto one knee. His brown eyes swim in the ocean blue eyes again as he opens the box. "Jonathan Lee Dennis, will you marry me?"

***

Big Fat Liar

The blue eyes couldn't stop staring into the mirror at himself. Seeing himself in a suit still surprises him. The fact he's about to get married in a few moments make his nerves flare. His pale fingers run through his brown hair and then tap on the vanity of Jonathan's grandmother. His nails are painted a pitch black, like his tux. The electric blue bow tie makes his eyes stand out, along with the eyeliner his sister added earlier. The tie is the same one Evan got him for his 32nd birthday; it's also the one he wore when Evan proposed to him. Jonathan's eyes wonder outside to the beautiful field of sunflowers his grandmother owns and wear he's about to be united with his love for the rest of his life. His mind runs wild like the sunflowers; how did the clown get so lucky? Evan's the sweetest thing on Earth and Jonathan is the most stubborn, but Evan could be sometimes as well. Jonathan has lied to Evan multiple times... Jonathan's lied to himself; about his feelings. Jonathan himself is a big fat liar. Jonathan didn't love himself before because he couldn't love anybody; it was because nobody showed him how to love himself. Evan Fong came into the rescue, even though he said multiple times, "Delirious doesn't need someone else to show him that he's amazing and very attractive."

Speaking of big fat liars, Evan would be one if he said he isn't nervous at this very moment. Behind these wooden doors sat multiple friends and family of both Dennis and Fong. They would watch Evan with his parents and then Jonathan with his. His heart couldn't take it; too many emotions were overflowing his mind. Vows. Remember. Evan spent hours writing them and then memorizing them. Suddenly the door swings open and Brock peeks his head out, "It's go time my man." Brock hugs him tightly before sneaking back in. Evan takes a deep breath, exhales, and releases all the crazy thoughts from his head.

Jonathan's mother pulls him from his grandmother's bedroom and leads him to the back doors, which were already opened. Jonathan's heart nearly jumps out of his chest.

Evan's black dress shoes make the slightest crunch noise in the grass. He steps in time with the music playing over the speakers inside Grandma Dennis's house. Before he knows it, he's standing under the arc of tied sunflowers. The smell abates his anxiety a bit. As soon as he meets those blue eyes though, all fear floods out of him, like Jonathan is the quiet before a storm. The smile that appears across his face makes Evan's knees weak as he smiles back.

His hands are very soft and cold to the touch of Evan's hands. Jonathan rubs the knuckles of the tan hands. A smile connects them both as they listen to their last minute priest Tyler Wine. "Through sickness and hell, whoops, I mean health…" everyone chuckles at the pig as he joins the couple in his own way. "You may now kiss the dork!" Tyler slams the book shut at throws his hands in the air as the two move in for a kiss. Evan's hand runs up Jonathan's neck and up through his sweet smelling hair.

Evan and Jonathan run into the sunflower field as everyone else rushes to get food. Their hands hold on tight to each other as they swing back and forth through the field. Jonathan chuckles as Evan nearly trips over something. Soon they both tumble into a patch of sunflowers. Their laughter echoes throughout the flowers. They lay together, their hands still together and smiles still plastered on their faces. The only difference is the fact both of their hands now had a ring on their fingers.

The cake is now cut by Jonathan. He snickers before smashing the cake into Evan's face. The guest erupt in laughter as Evan takes the same piece slipping off his face and smashes it into Jonathan's. Luckily their suits were both owned and not rented.

A few songs into the reception and Jonathan is handed his newborn niece. Remember that surprise Samuel and Megan were supposed to have for Jonathan? This tiny baby is the surprise; little Cassie. He swings around with her as Billy Joel plays over the speakers. Evan watches from a distance smiling. Delirious's face is full of joy as his thumb his grabbed by Cassie. She giggles when he makes silly faces and sings in a weird voice. A sudden warmth bursts through Evan's chest as he watches his newly wed play with his niece; a newborn. Thoughts swarm the brain of the owl, making him blush on the outside.

People wave and kiss the couple goodbye as they start toward the new jeep of Jonathan's. He's clear to drive. He suddenly picks up Evan bridal style and walks the rest of the way toward the blue vehicle. Jonathan turns around one last time for them both to wave to their friends and family. Delirious places Vanoss down so he can get in himself.

They wave one last goodbye before Jonathan starts their new beginning at Toronto, Canada, together.

Life will get better.

Even if you're fat.

Skinny.

Gay.

Straight.

Someone will see you one day and try their damnedest to get to know you or to just be with you.

Some people just get that person sooner than others.

Be patient.

An Evan will come tumbling along to you.

They'll show you that your stretch marks are the best thing about you.

Your teeth are perfect the way they are.

Your eye color is the best in the whole world.

The way you sleep is adorable.

The way you smile nearly kills them every time you do.

You will be loved, and I'd be called a big fat liar if I said no one will ever love you.

*** The End